The Highlander's Accidental Marriage

A MARRIAGE MART MAYHEM NOVEL

The Highlander's Accidental Marriage

A MARRIAGE MART MAYHEM NOVEL

CALLIE HUTTON

Entangled Publishing, LLC
2614 South Timberline Road
Suite 109
Fort Collins, CO 80525
Visit our website at www.entangledpublishing.com.

Scandalous is an imprint of Entangled Publishing, LLC.

Edited by Erin Molta
Cover Design by Heidi Stryker
Cover Art by Shutterstock

ISBN 978-1-68281-060-6

Manufactured in the United States of America

First Edition November 2015

To my furry friends: Madison, Angel, and Daisy, who keep me company (usually right under my feet) while I write away.

Chapter One

B raeden McKinnon glanced up at the sky at the light
drizzle and menacing clouds gathering. "I hope we
make it to the inn before the skies open up." His voice
carried in the wind to Monty Blackwood riding beside him,
both of their horses covered with sweat from the hard ride.

"Ach, it won't be the first time we've gotten soaked."

"Nay. And not the last," Braeden said. They continued
on for several minutes, the wind whipping around them
preventing any type of conversation.

They'd been on the road from Edinburgh University
for most of the morning. Braeden was on his way home to
the northwestern Highlands and Monty to his on the east
coast. Although the difference in their ages spanned two
decades, they were close friends and fellow professors at the

esteemed school.

At twenty-eight, Braeden was the youngest full professor at Edinburgh and, indeed, probably in all of Scotland and England. As odd as the situation was, given his superior intellect, he'd always been more comfortable with those much older than him.

"What is that up ahead?" Monty pulled on the reins to slow his horse at the sight of two women standing at the side of the road. One woman had her arm around the other, obviously comforting her.

"'Tis the middle of nowhere. What the devil are they doing?" Monty's brow furrowed as they came to a complete halt.

Braeden slid from his horse and strode to the women. "What happened, lasses?"

The wee one, with huge hazel eyes and dark brown curls tumbling around her ears continued to pat the other one on the back. "We had an accident." Her voice came out breathless and shaky. Her pale features and wide eyes registered shock.

"What sort of an accident?" Monty said as he joined them.

The other lady, older and obviously the employer of the tiny maid, wailed. "Our carriage slid in the mud, and then hit that boulder." She pointed to the massive protrusion a bit farther down. "And then…and then…" She buried her head into her maid's neck.

Her speech told him the ladies were from England—far from home.

The maid once again patted the older woman on the back. "It's all right. Just try to calm yourself." She turned to Braeden. "Both of us were thrown from the carriage when the door swung open after it hit the boulder. But the carriage went over the side. I'm terribly afraid the driver and footman, along with the poor horses, might have been injured. Or perhaps even killed."

The little bit of drizzle had turned into a steady rain. The only shelter was a copse of trees a short distance from the road. "Why don't ye lasses move over under those trees? Monty and I will see what we can learn about yer driver and footman."

"We shouldn't be talking to them, it is not proper." The older woman kept her back to them, but her whispered words reached him anyway.

"Madam, we are not standing in a London ballroom, I'm afraid. Ye need to get yerselves out of the rain and let us take a look at the carriage. If it makes ye feel better, I am Professor Braeden McKinnon, and this is Professor Monty Blackwood. We're both scholars at Edinburgh University." Realizing the women were distraught, he softened his voice. "I ken this is not a formal introduction, but 'tis the best we can do for now."

"They're Scottish!" the older woman said.

"Yes, dear, we are in Scotland, remember?" The wee one tilted her lips in a slight smile at Braeden. He shook his head at the nonsense London ladies were wont to spout off.

"See, now all is fine. Let us go out of the rain and allow the men to do what they need to." Thank goodness the young maid had a great deal more sense than her employer. She urged the older woman toward the copse of trees.

He stared after them. By the saints, even with her wet hair plastered to her forehead and the rain dripping from her pert nose, the lass was beautiful. Though tiny, she had curves in all the right places. His hands itched to run over the dips and rises of her body. *Ach!* He didn't usually have such a fascination for a lass.

Monty nudged him out of the trance the lass had put him into, and they set off toward the edge of the cliff. The climb down the hill where the carriage lay at the bottom was difficult with the rain making the descent slippery and hazardous. Grasping onto roots and branches, they cautiously made their way down.

The carriage lay on its side, broken parts of it scattered around the rocky spot where it had landed. It didn't take much to note that both the driver and footman had perished in the crash. Monty reluctantly drew his pistol and shot one of the two horses who hadn't died but was seriously injured.

"We'll have to send someone back to retrieve the bodies," Braeden said.

"Aye. But what will we do about the lasses?"

"Not much we can do. We can't leave them by the side of the road. We'll have to get them to the nearest inn so they can make arrangements to continue with their journey."

Braeden eyed the large trunk still strapped to the back of the broken carriage. "I imagine the lasses will want their belongings. Mayhap we can haul that trunk up for them."

"For what purpose? We can't set it on the backs of our horses. Let whoever comes for the bodies bring it back to the inn for them."

"A good idea." Braeden reached for a strong-looking branch and hauled himself up. After slipping and sliding their way back up the muddy hill, both men reached the top.

The young maid had left the older lady under the trees while she peeked over the edge of the cliff. "Are they dead?" Her tangled mass of wet hair spilled over her shoulders, almost blocking his vision of her lovely face. 'Twas too bad a beauty such as her was stuck tending to an older, and most likely complaining, Englishwoman.

"Aye, I'm afraid so, lass."

Tears filled her eyes as she took in the news. "How horrible. Their families must be notified."

"Where is it ye and yer lady are traveling?"

The lass seemed to shake herself from deep thought and regarded him. "We are traveling to the northwestern Highlands."

"Monty and I can take the two of ye to the nearest inn where ye can make whatever arrangements ye need."

"Yes, that would be wonderful. Thank you so much." She started to move away, and then turned back to him. Once more he was struck by her loveliness. She chewed on her lower lip, making him wish to cover the plumpness with his mouth.

What the devil is wrong with me?

"One thing, sir. Would it be possible to bring the trunk up here?"

"Now, lass. What good would that do ye? Surely ye can wait until whoever comes back here for the bodies to bring the trunk to ye," Monty said.

"Oh, no. Highwaymen could come by and riffle through our things. There are jewels in that trunk that cannot be left behind."

"Lass, we've only two horses—for two of us and two of ye. 'Tis enough of a burden without expecting the poor animals to carry a trunk." Braeden removed his spectacles and wiped the water from his eyes.

"Of course not." She raised her chin. Lord, she was a

bonny little thing. Her eyes flashed as if she stood several feet above him, instead of barely coming up to his chin. "I will merely remove a few pieces that should not be left behind."

Braeden glanced over at Monty who rolled his eyes.

"Aye. We'll haul it up here for ye." Braeden reached out to grab a branch and headed back down the trail.

With a great deal of groaning and swearing, they managed to get the trunk off the carriage and drag it up to the road and over to where the ladies sat under the trees. The rain continued its relentless assault, chilling him to the bone. The lasses must have been even worse off with their small size, especially the tiny maid.

Braeden set his hands on his hips, panting from the climb. "Here ye are. I suggest ye get what ye need and make it fast. Ye'll both be suffering from the ague if we don't get out of this rain."

The older lady continued to wail and moan as the maid opened the trunk only far enough to reach her hand in. She drew out a small pouch and proceeded to open it and don necklaces, bracelets, and rings, one after another. Her employer must have been quite lenient to allow her to adorn herself with the lady's jewels.

Wiping her forehead with the back of her bejeweled hand to push the ringlets plastered there, she continued to loop jewelry over her neck until she looked like a gypsy he had once seen at a fair. Both men stood watching her as she slid her hand in once again and dragged out a gown. Standing up, she pulled it over her head.

It wasn't until she had pulled on several more garments and draped them around her that Braeden's attention was caught. "How is it for a maid ye have so many frocks?"

"A maid?" The older woman exclaimed. She stood and straightened her shoulders, looking him in the eye. "How dare you, sir!"

Braeden and Monty exchanged surprised glances.

The outraged woman pointed to the wee lass. "I will have you know this is Lady Sarah Lacey, sister to the Duke of Manchester."

The little minx smiled at him and shimmied into another gown.

Sarah smirked. So the young handsome one—who'd introduced himself as Professor McKinnon—with the piercing blue eyes covered with spectacles that he kept wiping with his fingers, thought she was a maid? How amusing. His strong features and black wavy hair that skimmed his forehead put him in a class of men she'd spent a lot of time avoiding the last few years.

Tamping down the fluttering in her stomach, Sarah continued to drop one gown after another over her head until she no longer had the ability to move her arms. Of course, they were all getting ruined by the rain, but perhaps Alice could salvage most of them when they reached an inn. Leaving them at the bottom of that trail had not been a choice.

Hopefully, there was an inn nearby. She was soaked to the skin and wanted nothing more than a fireplace, a hot bath, and a cup of tea. Blasted Highlands. If it wasn't her twin sister she was traveling over this godforsaken land to see, she would turn right around and go home. She missed Sybil so much. Since her twin had married a Scotsman—a Scotsman!—Sarah had no choice if she wanted to see her new niece or nephew born. That was if she made it on time. This debacle would certainly delay them.

"Are ye done, lass? With the weight of me, ye, and all those wet clothes on my horse's back, we'll be lucky to make the next inn by nightfall."

She smiled at him. "Yes. I am ready." Without another word, she sashayed over to his horse and stood next to it, her eyebrows raised. "Well. Are we leaving?"

Professor McKinnon had to shut his mouth, which hung open. He stomped over and, grasping her waist, flung her onto the horse's back. She immediately began to slide to the other side, the weight of the wet clothes pulling her over. He reached out and grabbed her, tugging her the other way. Her arms flailing, she slid toward him and fell off, landing on him, sending both of them into the mud.

She lay sprawled on top of his muscular body, not more than an inch from his surprised expression. Mud splattered his spectacles as well as the rest of his face. Unable to help herself, she burst out laughing. He glowered at her and then his muscles relaxed, a slight smile teasing his lips, which turned into a grin. "I'd love to lie here with ye on top of me, lass, but I dinna think we'll get very far if ye do. 'Tis not fond of an audience, I am."

Red-faced, Sarah scrambled off him, the layers of wet clothes making her every move awkward.

"I'm so happy yer enjoying yourself with the lass, McKinnon, but my verra bones are beginning to get wet." Professor Blackwood groused.

"Yay. 'Tis right. We need to move along." Professor McKinnon rose from his mud bath and grasped her waist once more. "Yer very slippery, lass. So be careful as I place ye on my horse."

"That's the trouble, sir. You didn't place me on your horse. You tossed me like a sack of flour." Heat rose to her face when she realized his hands still held her as they had this exchange. Her heart sped up, and she felt the heat radiating from his body, despite how wet they both were.

"Lad, do ye suppose we could move along? Ye can have all the conversations ye wish with the lass once we are out of this blasted weather." Blackwood spoke over his shoulder as he gingerly placed Alice on his horse.

Without another word, the young professor placed her gently on the horse's back and climbed up behind her. Having had years of experience riding astride—as her sisters did as well—Sarah was comfortable with her position. However, she usually rode in breeches, and having all the wet, soggy gowns wrapped around her legs hindered any familiar posture she could assume.

Her head jerked back as Professor McKinnon moved the horse forward.

"We have to go slow since the muddy roads are dangerous, as ye've found out. 'Tis sorry I am for it, lass, but I'm afraid ye won't be out of this cold rain for a bit." The feel of his soft warm breath on her neck started goose bumps rising on her skin.

"If ye lean back against me, it would make the ride a bit warmer for both of us."

Her mother would be scandalized. Not only was she riding in front of a stranger, her bottom was secure against the part of him of which no innocent miss should be aware. The many layers of clothing provided not much of a buffer between their bodies.

Now he wanted her to rest against him? She should certainly give him a setdown for suggesting such a thing. But he had, after all, rescued them. And, truth be known, he had been a very good sport about dragging her trunk up and when she had laughed at him after she'd tumbled them both into the mud. But the wind blowing on them, along with her wet clothes, made the ride downright miserable. *Well, mother, some things simply cannot be helped.*

With that thought, she eased her body back until she touched his muscled chest. She held herself stiffly, not wanting to get too comfortable. *My, I feel warmer already.* In fact, she wouldn't be surprised if she saw steam rising from where their bodies met.

Now that she had acquiesced, he wrapped his arm around her waist and tugged her closer, chuckling in her ear. "Lass, ye have so many garments on, no one would be shocked. Relax."

Almost as if he'd read her mind.

"Do you know how far the next inn is?"

"I've been this way many times, and if I am correct, we should be near The Bush Inn. Mayhap no more than three quarters of an hour or so."

Her back tingled with the vibrations from his voice. Deep and solid. Just like the rest of him. He'd mentioned he and his travel companion were professors at Edinburgh University. He appeared terribly young for such a spot. He seemed only a few years her senior. Maybe she had misunderstood him.

Now that they were nearing the inn, she had to decide what she could do about her travel plans. No doubt she and Alice would require a day or two to recover from this mishap. That is if they didn't come down with an ague that prevented them from continuing on for longer. Luckily, she'd always had a strong constitution, but she couldn't say the same for her maid. Alice had been a last-minute substitution, because her own lady's maid had returned to her family's home for a funeral.

With no carriage, driver, or footman, they were certainly in a quandary. Yet, she had no intention of turning back. They would need to rent a carriage to take them home, anyway, so why not rent one to carry them on to Bedlay Castle?

The professor held out his arm. "Beyond that bend is the inn."

"Not too soon, to be sure," she said. She'd begun to shiver miles back and now she felt as if icicles dripped from her chin. Thankfully, the rain had turned to a light drizzle.

Even though it was only late afternoon, the sky was dark, and the lights from the inn glowed brightly, already making her feel warmer as they approached. Her escort brought the horse to a halt and slid down, handing the reins to a young stableboy. He reached up for Sarah and lifted her off. She continued to shake and shiver, almost unable to walk.

"Are ye all right, lass?"

"I th-th-think so."

Professor Blackwood and Alice were already hurrying to the door. Sarah took one step and stumbled. With the cold, the extra clothes, and the long ride, her legs wouldn't hold her, and she began to slide to the ground. He scooped her up and headed to the door.

"Put me down. This is most improper."

"Aye, and I assume falling flat on yer face is the proper thing for an English lady to do?" His grin told her he wasn't taking it at all seriously. If anyone she knew was in this inn, she would be ruined.

He nudged the door open with his hip and entered the room. "'Tis always amazing to me what ladies think is important."

"Not just ladies, sir. All of Polite Society casts dispersions on a woman who is viewed as being easy with her reputation. I assure you, I have no desire to shame my family by having my virtue come into question."

Professor McKinnon came to an abrupt stop. "Yer virtue?"

She raised her chin. "Indeed. Now put me down and kindly lower your voice."

Her feet landed on the floor with a thump. To her utter humiliation, her legs threatened to give way again. She shot him a grateful smile when he extended his arm so she could hold onto it. She tried hard to ignore his grin. Did the man not take anything seriously?

"Professor! So nice to see you." A barreled-chested man hurried down the stairs. "Are ye in need of a room?"

"Yes, Barton, two rooms, in fact."

"Aye. Yer lucky I have two rooms left. One for ye and one for the other two?" He gestured with his head toward Alice and Professor Blackwood.

"Nay. One for me and the other fellow, and one for the ladies."

Sarah felt the heat rise from her toes all the way to her face at the suggestion that she and this stranger would be sharing a room. At the same time, a previously unknown feeling settled in her middle at the thought of her and this handsome professor climbing into bed together.

Well, I've finally done it. I've managed to shock myself.

"I'd say by the look of ye that a warm fire and one of my wife's meat pies would help ye out."

"May I have a bath sent up, please?" Sarah moved away from Professor McKinnon so the innkeeper would not think there was anything between them except a stranger helping a woman in trouble.

"Certainly, my lady. My wife will take ye to yer room and get ye settled."

"Thank you."

"I would appreciate a bath myself, Barton. If 'tis not too much trouble. I seem to have landed in a bit of mud." Mr. McKinnon grinned at Sarah, but then turned serious. "But first ye will need to send for the magistrate. It seems the ladies here were in a carriage that went over the Manfred cliff. Killed their driver and footman."

"*Ach.* 'Tis a dangerous place on the road, for sure. I'll have my boy go fetch him straightaway."

The innkeeper's wife led them all upstairs. Sarah was never so happy to see a clean room with a nice bright fire keeping the space warm. "Alice, I'm sorry for the mess I've made of my clothes. I'm afraid it will take some time for you to set them to rights. We may need to stay here for a couple of days before we move on."

"Move on, my lady? Surely you don't intend to continue? This is a cursed place."

"I do, indeed. You forget yourself, Alice. My sister lives in this 'cursed place,' and I had planned to see her and the new babe. That is precisely what I shall do. We'll need some time to make other arrangements and to notify my brother of the two deaths. Since they were not regular servants, he will need to seek out their families to claim the bodies."

A chastened Alice eased herself down to the edge of the small cot against the wall. "Oh, my lady. I don't know if I have the strength to carry on."

"Nonsense. All will be well. Now help me out of these gowns so I can prepare for my bath." There was a slight scratching at the door. "Ah, that must be the bath now."

Afterward, Sarah donned a clean, dry dress the innkeeper's wife had provided. While she'd bathed, Alice had dried her mistress's clothing in front of the fire and cleaned herself up with the warm water in the bowl on the dresser.

Feeling much better, Sarah sat while Alice twisted her mass of curls into a bun at the back of her neck, not bothering with letting it dry first.

"My lady, the gentlemen await you and your maid in the dining room for supper." Mrs. Barton arrived at their door just as Sarah and Alice were ready to proceed downstairs.

"Why would we eat with those men?" Alice frowned. "We aren't traveling with them."

"Alice, it is good manners. If they sent the invitation to us, it would be quite rude to refuse. After all, they did rescue us."

It was disconcerting to have a maid who had a stronger sense of propriety than she did. She and her sisters had oftentimes skirted some of the more rigid mores of Society — riding in breeches being one of them. Truth be known, if they were anywhere near London she would be more concerned herself, but they were in the wilds of Scotland where the chance of her running into anyone she knew was slight.

B raeden and Monty stood as the ladies approached the table. "Ye are looking much better, lass." Braeden pulled out a chair for Sarah. The smells coming from the kitchen had his mouth already watering.

"Yes. A hot bath and clean, dry clothes make a great deal of difference in how one views the world."

Mrs. Barton arrived along with her two young daughters. They set bowls of some type of fragrant stew, warm bread, butter, and cheese in front of them.

There was very little conversation while they ate, just comments on the good fare and their luck in being able to secure rooms.

Sarah wiped her mouth on the napkin and laid it along-side her plate. "Professor McKinnon. Something has occurred to me."

He leaned back in his chair and crossed his arms over his chest. "Aye. And what is that, lass?"

"Are you, by chance, a relative to Laird Duncan McKinnon of Dundas?"

Although startled by her question, he showed no surprise. "I am. The laird is my cousin. His da and mine were brothers."

"Do you live near him, then?"

"Indeed, I do. My family has been in service to the lairds for generations. My mum and da, along with my sisters, work at the castle. My brothers each have a patch of land they live on with their families. They're sheep farmers. When I am home from university, Duncan allows me to stay at Dundas to have access to the library."

He began to squirm as Sarah continued to smile at him. What was the lass up to now? For some reason he didn't think it would bode well for him.

Tilting his chair backward on two legs, with a niggle of concern deepening in his belly at the lass's expression, he asked, "Why do ye want to ken?"

"Because, sir, it relieves my mind quite a bit." She placed her hands in her lap and attempted to look very innocent.

He narrowed his eyes at her. "And why is that, lass?" Her innocent look didn't fool him. He'd already decided this lass was someone of whom he should be leery. She had quite a bit of pluck, unlike most English ladies he'd met.

"It so happens my sister, who I am on my way to visit, is married to Laird McKinnon's friend and neighbor, Laird Liam MacBride."

"Is she now?" He glanced over at Monty who shrugged his shoulders. "And just why does this relieve ye?"

"Because I will feel quite safe traveling with you the rest of the way to Bedlay Castle." She gave him a bright smile.

The front legs of his chair hit the floor with a thump. "What?!"

Chapter Two

B raeden stared at Lady Sarah openmouthed. Did this wee slip of a lass just announce she expected him to travel with her to Bedlay Castle?

"Yer mistaken, lass. I am not traveling to Bedlay Castle."

"No. But you are traveling home to Dundas, correct?"

"Aye."

"McKinnon lands border MacBride lands, correct?"

He nodded slowly. Surely the lass wasn't serious. In order for him to escort the ladies to Bedlay Castle he would have to rent a carriage, and the entire trip would take more than twice as long as he intended to be on the road.

The letter he was waiting for might have already arrived. He'd wanted to join this particular expedition to Rome for more than two years. Most of his fellow professors thought he was crazy to even attempt to secure the post because of his age. *His age.* A problem he'd dealt with many times over the years.

When the special tutor his da had arranged had told them that at thirteen years Braeden was ready for university, it had taken quite a bit of persuasion on both his and the tutor's part to convince his parents. *Too young.* He'd heard it all his life. Too young to read at three years, too young to do higher level mathematics at seven years. But he'd done it, and continued on. *Unusually superior intellect*, his tutor had said.

He needed this expedition to convince others that he belonged, even if he was decades younger than most in his field. He had to prove to them, as well as himself, that age did not matter when the passion for your work was as strong as his. This was not an opportunity he wanted to miss.

Then he looked at her face and knew the decision had been made. Hope burned in her eyes. Hope and uncertainty. For, as bold as the lass was, she knew he could easily say nay. Then where would that leave her? Forced to continue on or return home with just a maid and a rented carriage. His mum would knock him over the head if he abandoned a lady and left her to the dangers of the road with no protection.

He sighed. "Aye. I'll travel with ye as yer escort."

Monty stood and slapped him on the back. "Seeing as how I'm going in the opposite direction, I wish ye well. I'm heading off to bed to get an early start in the morning."

Lady Sarah clapped her hands. "Wonderful. Now we must make plans." She tapped her chin with a slim finger. "First we must rent a carriage. And, of course, I'll need a few days to get my clothing in order. Oh, and we'll need to see if my trunk is still where we left it. No matter if it isn't. There must be a shop nearby where I can purchase a few…" She stopped and stared at him. "What?"

Mouth agape, he regarded her with a combination of awe and fear. The wee lass brought to mind a small bird from America he'd read about. She was like the hummingbird, flitting about in her thoughts, giving orders, making decisions, and generally taking charge of a journey for which he should have control.

"Wait just a minute, here, lass. As for a carriage, that would be for me to secure. Clothing doesn't matter. As long as ye have something to cover yerself with, we need not worry about any additional items. And we are naught settling ourselves in here for a couple of days. I am expecting a very important letter to arrive at my home, and I intend to be there when it does."

She picked up on the one thing apparently dearest to her heart. "I will not continue on this journey without sufficient clothing."

He leaned back in his chair, eying her speculatively. "That depends on what ye deem 'sufficient.' To me, ye look fine right now." Aye, she did. Her eyes flashed, her chin was thrust forward, and her cheeks flushed bright red. Right now he wanted to taste those plump lips.

Merely to keep her from talking, of course.

"Fine?" She looked down at the frock. "This belongs to the innkeeper's daughter."

"I'll offer a coin to Mrs. Barton for the garment, and we'll be on our way."

She leaned toward him. If he didn't think she would bop him on the head, he would have laughed to see such a wee thing all worked up. "I will not leave here without enough clothes for at least a few days."

He shifted in his chair until he was almost nose-to-nose

with the hummingbird. "We will leave here when I am sure we have a carriage sturdy enough and horses hardy enough to last the journey."

She glared at him. He glared back.

S arah turned so Alice could unfasten the gown Mrs. Barton had lent her. "Honestly, I cannot understand that man. How can he possibly think we would be ready to continue on to Bedlay Castle without clothing? Never in my life have I met a more stubborn man."

Alice's nimble fingers worked the hooks and eyes. "My lady, perhaps we should be grateful that he's agreed to accompany us to your sister's home."

She sighed as the dress slid down her body, leaving her in only her chemise, since her stays were still wet. "I know, Alice, and believe me, I am grateful." She slipped into the worn linsey-woolsey nightgown, also borrowed from Mrs. Barton, and sighed. "He is handsome, though. Wouldn't you say?"

"Yes, my lady. Indeed he is a handsome chap."

"How can he be a professor at university? Professor Blackwood appears about twenty years older than McKinnon, but he didn't dispute him being a professor."

"I'm sure I don't know." Alice gathered up the clothes that had dropped to the floor. "I will see what I can do about the gowns that you managed to bring with you." She walked to where the garments were laid out in front of the fire. "Most of them are dry."

Sarah waved her hand. "Don't bother with them now,

Alice. Even if the dear professor insists on leaving as soon as he has secured a carriage, that will still take some time. You can deal with the clothing in the morning. Surely you are as tired as I am?"

"I am a bit worn." The maid eyed the small cot that had been set up in the corner of the room for her use.

"Then we will turn in, so I am ready to do battle in the morning with our traveling companion. Good night."

"Good night, my lady."

They both climbed into their respective beds. Sarah blew out the candle. She rolled onto her back and tucked her hands beneath her head. Immediately her thoughts turned to Professor Braeden McKinnon. Laird Duncan McKinnon's cousin.

She had been planning on traveling to the Highlands with Sybil when her twin had attended Laird McKinnon's wedding to their close friend, Lady Margaret. But an illness had kept Sarah from going. They'd all been surprised when Sybil sent a letter a few weeks later saying she was leaving Margaret's new home to spend time at Laird Liam MacBride's castle a short distance away.

Her brother, Drake, had not been happy with that turn of events, and had immediately planned a trip to fetch her back. He had been somewhat calmed when he received a letter from Liam, assuring him that Sybil would be well chaperoned, and he would provide her with safe passage home.

A second letter from Laird McKinnon, verifying Liam was an honorable man and would take good care of Sarah, had calmed her brother even further, although he had still threatened to travel to Scotland.

Like Sybil, Sarah had a distrust of Scottish men. From what she'd heard over the years, Scots were more interested in brawling, women, and drink. However, with McKinnon being so young and a professor, he couldn't have spent many years pursuing those nefarious activities.

She rolled over and hugged the pillow. What disturbed her most was her reaction to his touch. This was certainly the wrong time to become enamored with a man. She had her life planned out at least for the next few years. The encumbrance of a beau would not do.

With her first book about ready for publication, and with her publisher so certain it would be well received, she didn't need the distraction of a man, no matter how handsome he was.

Since she'd spent many hours behind closed doors filling up pages of foolscap with her stories, it had been easy to discourage suitors during her Seasons, because none of them had affected her the way Professor McKinnon did. It would certainly be in her best interests to keep the man as far from her as possible during this trip. She grinned at the memory of his surprise at how she'd taken control of the travel plans. He certainly hadn't appreciated her forwardness.

Yet, with his handsome visage and sense of humor, this could be a very pleasant trip. It had been a while since she was able to cross swords with someone who could keep up with her. As long as there was no more touching. None. At all.

Ever.

Despite his best efforts, it had taken Braeden two days to secure a sturdy carriage and horses he felt were robust enough to provide them with safe passage. During that time, he'd met on several occasions with Lady Sarah to finalize plans. The lass would make Boney a fine general. She had lists and demands and suggestions galore.

During one particularly trying session, he'd stuck a piece of bread into her mouth to get her to stop talking. He would have actually preferred to place his lips where her mouth was busy chattering, but that would not be a good idea. Instead of berating him as any other English lady would, she'd merely taken the bit of bread from her mouth, smiled, and said, "Thank you. I am quite hungry."

There seemed to be no way to deal with the lass. She was a firestorm of activity. True to her word, she uncovered a shop in the nearest town where she replaced the clothing she'd lost in the accident with items the shopkeeper had ready-made. She spent hours supervising the packing of said clothing, and she even consulted with Mrs. Barton on what the innkeeper served for dinner each evening.

"There you are, Professor. I've been looking for you." She hurried toward him, determination in every step.

"*Ach*, lass. 'Tis why I was hiding." He jumped up to pull out a chair for her at the table where he fiddled with a glass of ale.

"Nonsense. We must make sure all is ready to leave in the morning. I wonder how long it will take from here to Bedlay?"

He stared for a minute at a spot on the wall above her head. "With no delays, and allowing for meal stops, changing horses, and sleep, it will take four days, three hours, thirty-seven minutes. And that is only if the bridge in Ullapool is not closed due to flooding."

She gaped at him, her mouth open. "How did you do that?"

"Do what?"

"Arrive at such a precise answer without pen and paper?"

He shrugged. "I don't exactly know. It just sort of happens. But ye needn't fash yerself. 'Tis all ready. I am certain the carriage and horses are sturdy enough for the trip. If the weather is fine, I will ride my horse, Niels, alongside the carriage, so ye and yer maid can have yer privacy."

The lass shook her head, returning to their conversation. "Niels. That's an odd name for a horse."

"In Gaelic it means *champion*."

She leaned her elbows on the table—which he assumed was against proper English ladylike behavior—and smiled. "And *is* he a champion?"

"Aye. He's been mine for going on ten years. He might not have won races, but he has certainly carried me far and wide." He watched her over the rim of his glass as he took another sip of ale. "Do ye want something to drink, lass?"

She leaned back. "What are you drinking?

"Ale. Barton makes the best ale for miles around."

She wrinkled her wee nose, sending extra blood to certain parts of his body. "I think I will have a cup of tea."

After summoning one of the Barton daughters to bring tea, he once more turned his attention to this very intriguing lass. "Did the magistrate talk to ye about the footman and driver?"

She sighed. "Yes. I gave him the information he needed to contact my brother so he can make arrangements to have the bodies sent to Manchester Manor. I also sent a note to my brother, assuring him Alice and I were fine and would continue our journey under the protection of a university professor related to Laird McKinnon."

He grinned inwardly. Most likely her brother would assume this professor was many years beyond his age. The lass was indeed a clever one. "Aye. Manchester Manor is yer family home?" When she nodded, he continued, "Ye said yer brother is a duke?"

"Yes. The Duke of Manchester. He is married to a botanist, and they have a little boy, Robert, Marquess of Stafford, and a new baby girl, Lady Esther Lacey. I miss them already." She stirred cream and sugar into her tea, her countenance a bit more somber than it had been a few moments ago.

"Ye long for yer family, do ye?"

"I do. I have two married sisters back in England. My sister Abigail and her husband, Joseph, have twin boys, David and John. Marion and her husband, Tristan, have a little girl, Daisy Susan. They are wonderful children."

"And yer traveling to yet another sister?"

"Yes. My twin sister, Sybil." She blew lightly on her tea and took a sip.

His vision was captured by those tempting rosy lips. He imagined nibbling on them, then sucking and teasing until she opened so he could sweep in and taste the sweetness of her mouth. Stroke his tongue over her lips, touch various spots in the recesses of her mouth until he found which parts were sensitive. It took him a minute to realize she had continued speaking.

"She is about to have a baby. That is why I'm visiting."

"And one day ye will join yer sisters and have bairns of yer own." His face flushed at the thought of what she would do with a husband to create those bairns. How that husband would touch her silky skin, run his palms over her curves, touch her in places only a husband was permitted.

He was startled when his muscles tightened, refusing to believe it was what could only be called jealousy. That was absurd. Lady Sarah was a pleasant—albeit bossy—lass who needed his help. He had plans to complete when he arrived home and found a letter waiting for him. That was his focus. His work, not the pretty wee lass with the enticing lips.

"No babies for me."

"Nay?"

"No. I have nieces and nephews to dote on, with more on the way." She took another swallow of tea and stood. "I think I will check with Alice to make sure the packing is going well."

The sway of her hips as she walked away had him thinking once again of how lucky that future husband would be to crawl under the covers with Lady Sarah and her fine body.

Chapter Three

A light drizzle greeted the group as they left the inn and headed to the carriage Professor McKinnon had secured for them. The dark, dreary morning dampened Sarah's spirits, until he announced he would be joining her and Alice in the carriage to avoid the rain.

Excitement flooded her senses, and her heartbeat picked up, annoying her to no end. She did not want to be aware of the man. Indeed, not any man. The path she'd chosen, for at least the next few years, was set. Attraction to men was not part of it. Especially to one handsome Scot who would now be merely inches from her.

She and Alice took one side of the spacious carriage as their escort gave the driver final instructions. The vehicle shifted to one side as he climbed in and settled across from them. All the air left the carriage and her lungs as the spaciousness disappeared.

My goodness, he took up an enormous amount of room.

His knees almost bumped hers as he shifted in his seat, getting comfortable. Alice seemed completely unaware of the man's presence and continued to stare out the window, hiding a yawn behind her hand. How could her maid not notice the warm, hard body that had just plopped itself down, taking up so much of the space?

She certainly didn't need to be mindful of him, either. Reaching into the satchel at her feet, she pulled out a book. She opened it and stared at the page, her thoughts wandering.

"Lass, how can ye read without light?"

She slammed the book shut and glowered at him. Was he going to annoy her the entire trip? "I wasn't reading, I merely wanted to be sure my book was handy."

"Aye, I understand." He nodded at the book in her lap. "I believe 'twas upside down, too." The grin on his face told her he hadn't believed her lie. Hopefully, he didn't realize how much he disturbed her. Even in the dim light she could make out his handsome features. She'd known so few men who wore glasses. Rather than detract from his comely visage, the wire-framed spectacles added to it. As did the silky black curls that fell onto his forehead.

She took herself to task. This was ridiculous. It would be a very long, tiresome journey if she didn't get her emotions under control. It was so unlike her to react to a man.

The carriage started up with a jolt and then moved into a smooth cadence. Professor McKinnon had hired a driver and two footmen. When questioned about the extra man, he stated parts of the route they would travel were known to be plagued by highwaymen. She shivered, thinking of being confronted by robbers, which was why she'd put her jewelry in a sack underneath the seat.

"Are ye cold, lass?"

"No. I was just contemplating how frightening it would be if we were confronted by highwaymen."

"Nay. Dinna fash yerself. We have three men outside, and I have my pistol with me."

"Pistol? You are carrying a weapon?"

He reached into his jacket and withdrew a rather alarming gun.

"I hope you know how to use that."

"Aye, lass, and one bit of advice. Never carry a weapon you don't ken how to use or are afraid to use."

"I hope to never learn how to shoot a gun. Just the thought of hitting someone with a bullet makes my stomach roil." Carrying a gun and teaching at Edinburgh University did not seem to mix. Who was this man who had so captured her attention?

"Please excuse my rudeness, Professor McKinnon, but I can't help but notice you seem quite young to be a professor at Edinburgh University."

In the faint light the slow lazy smile he cast her almost stopped her breath.

"Aye. 'Tis not a rude question, lass. I hear it all the time. First, as ye pointed out, I am a tad young, so please call me Braeden. Professor McKinnon stands in front of a classroom. He doesn't ride in carriages with a beautiful lass."

Blushing despite trying to ignore his compliment, she said, "I'm not sure that is proper."

"*Ach.* There ye go again with yer English 'what is proper.' By necessity we will be spending a lot of time together over the next few days. I think, given those circumstances, we can dispense with the formality."

"Very well. But only in private. I don't want to give anyone the wrong impression."

He raised his eyebrows. "And that would be?"

Heat rose to her face as she thought of how improper her thoughts had been since she'd met the man. Why, oh why did he affect her so? It had to be the close proximity, because she'd never experienced these strange feelings, nor had these disturbing thoughts before, with any other man.

"In Polite Company gentlemen and ladies do not use their given names when addressing each other."

"Ah. So we are not in polite company now? 'Tis impolite company? Should I hurl insults at ye, then?"

The quick retort on her lips faded as she caught the sparkling humor in his eyes. She would have to remember that, despite his serious appearance, he enjoyed teasing her.

"No. No need to hurl insults. But you have not answered my question. How is it you are a professor at such an esteemed institution?"

She shifted to rest one booted foot on his opposite knee. "I don't understand it myself. It seems out of mum and da's six bairns, I was blessed—or cursed—with unusual intelligence." He looked out the window at the slowly lightening sky. "Ever since I can remember, I've had this thirst for knowledge. I taught myself to read by mimicking my sisters. When I outgrew the castle tutor, da hired a special one for me. He took me as far as he could and then told my parents I was ready for university."

"How old were you?"

"Thirteen years," he said wryly.

"That explains how you were able to calculate in your head our arrival at Bedlay." She tilted her head, examining him, trying to understand this man who had captivated her so. "How did it feel?"

He apparently knew exactly what she had asked. "Frightening at times. There were occasions when I wanted to push away all the numbers and words racing around my brain and just tend the sheep with my brothers." He shrugged. "It never worked."

"And what do you teach?"

"Classical archeology with a focus on Ancient Rome."

He chuckled as she slowly repeated the words. "*Ach*, lass. Ye say it like there's something nasty on yer tongue."

"I don't mean to. I guess it's that I don't really know what 'classical archeology' is."

"According to how the books read, classical archeology is the study of civilizations of the Mediterranean, as well as the Ancient Greek and Roman cultures."

"That is indeed a mouthful, Professor."

He smiled slowly. "Braeden."

Once more, heat rose to her face as his deep voice rolled over her, making it even worse when he grinned. Apparently, the light was enough now that he could see her face quite well. Something tickled her belly when he said his name. Soft and low, as if he murmured into her ear in the dark.

What in heaven's name is wrong with me?

What the devil is wrong with me? Braeden was having a difficult time keeping his eyes off Sarah. Not that it was an easy chore, anyway, since they sat only a few feet from each other. But every expression on her lovely face had him wanting to tug her across the space and plop her onto his lap.

Now that he'd been subjected to several of her regal looks and highborn comments, he couldn't believe that at their first meeting he had thought she was a maid. Though, all that comforting she'd been doing with the other woman when they had come upon them on the road had certainly cast her in that light. Sarah was a wee bonny lass, but a strong woman. No swooning and tears for her.

Most lasses who had been through what she'd suffered—a serious accident, terrible weather, and a loss of her servants and carriage—would have taken to their beds for a week. Yet the hummingbird had cajoled him into escorting them to Bedlay Castle, bullied her maid into getting everything done in a timely manner, and had tried very hard to take control of the entire journey. She was certainly a lass to admire.

And admire her he did. Her tiny form displayed enough womanly curves that there was no question as to her being a lass full grown. Her soft mouth begged to be covered by a man who knew what he was about and ready to teach her the art of kissing. Right now she studied him under thick eyelashes with bright eyes that danced with intelligence and humor. Aye, Lady Sarah was a sight to behold.

And it would be wise to use his intelligence to avoid any further involvement with her. He had his plans all set. A lass was not part of the design.

"How did you become interested in archeology?"

Glad to be able to focus on his work instead of Sarah, he said, "From the time I was a lad I enjoyed visiting the crumbling ruins of castles and keeps scattered throughout the Highlands. When my da had the time—which was rare—

he would take me miles and miles from home to investigate some remnants of a clan's home."

"Are there so many?"

"Aye." His stomach tightened at the number of homes abandoned to the elements with their clans moving to America and Canada after the Clearances. His clan was indeed lucky to hold onto their land and continue to provide a living for its members.

"The Clearances did their damage to many clans."

"Ah. Yes. I remember that from my history lessons." She shook her head, tendrils of dark curls bouncing from where they'd gotten loose from her bun. "Not something my country did that I'm proud of, I'm afraid."

"'Tis a comforting thought coming from a Sassenach."

"A what?"

"Sassenach."

"I never heard that word before, but I have a feeling it's not a compliment."

"It means 'outlander' or someone who doesn't belong."

"*Hmm.* I'm not sure I like that."

"Actually, I don't like it, either. I think there is nowhere on this earth you would not belong, Sarah." Once again her face flushed, and he could have bitten his tongue. Why did he insist on bantering with the lass? It would be better for his peace of mind to ride Niels alongside the carriage—as soon as the weather cleared up. Remove himself from her disturbing presence before he did something stupid.

The sun had burned off the clouds by the time they stopped for tea. Sarah stretched as the carriage came to a rolling stop, attempting to ease the muscles in her neck. Aside from feeling the necessity for food, her muscles needed to move. Not used to sitting for long periods of time, she was anxious to take a brisk walk before she ate.

"I will join you in a few minutes." She called over her shoulder as she started off in the opposite direction of the inn.

"Lass, where are ye going?" Braeden hurried up alongside her.

"I must walk for a bit. I am very sore from sitting so many miles."

"Not by yerself." He extended his arm, his eyebrows lifted in challenge.

"Indeed? And what manner of trouble do you suppose I would encounter right outside this inn that I need to be accompanied by a man?" She smirked and placed her fingertips on his arm.

"Ye never ken, lass, and that little bit of holding on is good enough for yer fancy ballrooms, but the ground here is unsteady. I'll not have ye stumbling and hurting yerself." He took hold of her hand and tucked it securely in his arm.

"What do you know of fancy ballrooms? Have you been to London?"

"Aye. I have a friend I visited a few years back. He took me to a couple of yer social events. 'Twas quite an experience."

"In what way?"

He gazed out at the surroundings, taking a moment to answer her question. "The lasses were sweet, but I was truly frightened by their mums."

Sarah burst out laughing. "It didn't take you long to realize *ton* mamas are the most fierce animals in all of England. If there are young ladies to be married off, a mama's job is to make sure she makes the best match possible for her daughter's station."

"Aye. I guess 'tis true in Scotland as well. At least in Edinburgh, that is. Marriage is contracted a bit differently away from the large cities, unless yer a laird, in which case the selection of a bride is a serious business."

"Lady Margaret—your cousin Duncan's bride—married a man her parents had selected. I assume Laird McKinnon had to give that a great deal of thought. I often wondered why he agreed to marry an Englishwoman."

"Yet yer sister married a Scotsman, as well."

She nodded. "And quite a surprise it was to us all."

They strolled for a few more minutes, each occupied with his or her own thoughts. Braeden slowly turned them so they headed toward the inn. "I don't know about ye, lass, but my stomach could use some food."

"I agree. I could also use a cup of tea."

"Nay. A tankard of ale."

They grinned at each other as they made their way back to the inn.

She was enjoying herself, and it troubled her. She found it very easy—much too easy—to talk to Braeden. The warmth from his body where her arm rested felt comforting and disturbing at the same time. She'd strolled Hyde Park, London ballrooms, and the theater, too many times to count, with an arm linked together with a gentleman. Never had she been so entirely aware of a man. Or found such comforting warmth from his touch.

It had always been easy to hold herself apart from her potential suitors, to remind herself of her intention to concentrate on her writing. She'd hoped to one day have the book she'd been working on actually published.

She'd kept her writing a secret from her family, even her twin. This was something that belonged to her alone. As much as she loved her family, there were times when she'd felt the need to stand out. To not be just one of the Lacey girls, or one half of a set of twins. It had been important to have something of her very own.

She had started with a journal when she was still in the schoolroom. Soon she began to make up stories in her head to lull herself to sleep at night. The next step, writing down those stories, ended with her penning the words "The End" and realizing she'd actually completed a book. A romance story about two people she'd conjured up from her imagination.

It had been a heady feeling.

Since her aspirations had come true, she had no interest in the professor as far as marriage was concerned, but he certainly had her thinking other things upon which an innocent miss should not be dwelling.

Years ago, she and Sybil had snatched a book from her brother Drake's room. Their older sisters had done the same thing; it seemed to be a rite of passage for the Lacey girls. The drawings in the book—with ladies and gentlemen in various, and truly awkward, positions—had made them giggle and blush. Why she was thinking of that book now and the scandalous images, as Braeden walked so close to her, certainly gave her pause.

She must stop this fascination with the man. He had agreed to accompany her and Alice to Bedlay Castle, where he would leave them in Liam's care and travel on to his home. Never to see her again.

A dismal thought.

Dismal because, she quickly assured herself, they were becoming friends. That was all. They had developed an easy friendship, and she would miss him when they parted, just like she had missed Lady Margaret when she'd left for her wedding.

That was all. Truly.

"My lady, the innkeeper has tea ready if you will follow me to the dining room." Alice met them at the door and directed them to a small room off the common area. A fire burned brightly in the fireplace where a table with two place settings had been arranged. Sarah turned to her maid. "Have you eaten, Alice?"

"Yes, my lady. I would like to take a walk for some exercise."

"Be sure to take one of the footmen with ye," Braeden said as he held out the chair for Sarah.

Sarah liked the way Braeden looked out for the women. He wasn't treating them as if they were a bother. It said a lot about his character.

Tea was not as good as at the last inn. Sarah pushed aside most of the food on her plate, but had two cups of tea, which satisfied her.

"No wonder yer so tiny, lass. Ye eat no more than a bird."

"Not usually. In fact I have a very good appetite, even for a lady." She grinned. "However I find the tea much better than the food."

"I'm afraid yer correct. 'Twas not the best, but ye need

to keep up yer strength."

She raised her eyebrows. "Why? Do you intend to have me pull the carriage this afternoon?"

Braeden threw back his head and shouted with laughter. "Ye do have a sense of humor, Sarah."

She jerked at his use of her name. It rolled off his tongue in that Scottish sort of way, softly, with a burr, making her stomach clench and her face heat. Goodness, she was about to make a fool of herself over a man she'd met only a few days ago. Why in heaven's name did it have to be a man whose company she was forced to endure for the next several days who set her heart to pumping?

"My mother always said a sense of humor will get you through many a difficult situation."

"And being in my company is so difficult, then?" His smooth voice, the slight tilt of his lips, with those deep blue eyes peering at her from behind his spectacles, was enough to spur her into action.

She rose on unsteady legs. "I think I would like to visit the necessary before we leave." Her face grew even warmer at his chuckle as she turned and left the room.

Does he find me so amusing, or does he guess my thoughts?

Chapter Four

"I will be riding Niels this afternoon since the weather is so fine. It will also give ye more room in the carriage," Braeden said as he assisted Sarah into the vehicle.

Both grateful and disappointed at his decision, Sarah chastised herself and pulled out a stack of pages she had written for her next book. Based on the success of Jane Austen's novels, Sarah's publisher seemed to think Sarah's book would be a success as well, and was anxious for her to complete another one.

The carriage was not conducive to writing, so it was a good time to go over what she'd written so far. It would also help get her mind off the handsome Scotsman and focus on what was important to her, and the pleasure of seeing her sister soon.

"My lady, 'tis quite hot in the carriage. May I roll up the flaps?"

Sarah looked up from her manuscript at her maid. "Yes,

of course." She peered closer. "Do you feel all right, Alice? You look a little peaked."

"I am just a bit overwarm. I think I will remove my jacket."

"You do seem a bit flushed. Perhaps all the excitement has overset you."

"Perhaps." Alice unfastened her jacket and laid it carefully on the bench next to her. "I think a short nap might restore me."

"Excellent. I find naps and tea the best cure for most anything." Sarah returned to her work and reviewed the same paragraph for the third time. No sooner had she begun to read than Braeden passed by the carriage, visible from the flap Alice had opened. The man certainly sat a horse well. The firm muscles of his thighs gripped the horse, and when he rode forward, the sight of his muscled backside had her agreeing with Alice that it was indeed warm in the carriage.

She shook her head and returned to her work.

Alice had been sleeping more than an hour when a loud crack sounded and the carriage began to tilt. Had they had another accident? Placing her papers aside, Sarah used both hands to grab the metal handle near the oil lamp and held on. "Alice. Alice. Wake up before you're tossed around like a cloth doll."

The maid sat up, her eyes wide as she grabbed the handle right above her head. "What happened now?"

"I'm not sure, but the carriage is coming to a halt. There was a crack, so I'm thinking perhaps one of the wheels has broken." They continued to rock as the carriage slowed and then stopped at an odd angle.

"My lady, this trip has been disastrous. Perhaps the good Lord is warning us to return home to England. It appears

Scotland is not for us."

"Don't be silly, Alice. I'm sure the good Lord has more things to take up his time and attention than worrying about our trip to see Sybil."

"Lasses, are ye all right?" Braeden flung open the carriage door, concern written clearly on his face.

"Yes, we're fine. A somewhat bumpy ride near the end, but all is well. What happened?" She released the handle and worked the muscle in her hand which ached from clasping the handgrip so tightly.

"One of the smaller front wheels cracked. It will take some time to travel back to the last town we passed to get this one fixed or secure another one."

Sarah chewed on her lip. "Will we be safe sitting out here waiting? Didn't you mention highwaymen?"

"Dinna fash yerself, lass. This area is not known for highwaymen, but I'll send one of the footmen with the wheel, and I'll stay here with ye both."

Sarah made to climb out of the carriage. "Oh, dear, I can't help but wonder what my sister will think with all these delays."

Braeden helped her down, and she shook out her skirts, looking around the area. It was a heavily wooded spot. Despite his assurances, this was indeed a place where robbers would have plenty of opportunities to hide themselves and accost travelers on the road. She shivered, wondering if Alice was correct and the good Lord wanted her back in the safety of her brother's home.

Nonsense.

"Alice, you might as well come out and stretch your muscles. It appears we will be here a while."

When the maid didn't answer, Sarah stuck her head in the carriage. "Alice?"

The woman's eyes were closed again, and they popped open as Sarah leaned into the carriage and spoke. "What is the matter?"

"Nothing, my lady. Just a bit tired from all the travel." Alice climbed out of the carriage blinking at the sun.

"Lass, you do look peaked. Perhaps you should sit over there, under the shade of those trees." Braeden pointed to an area off the road that looked inviting.

Alice reached out to grasp Sarah's hand. She assisted the maid to the tree stump and got her settled. She returned to where Braeden was helping strap the damaged wheel to the second horse and giving the footman final instructions. She looked at the broken wheel, marveling at their bad luck thus far.

Once the footman was on his way, Sarah said, "Please take a walk with me."

Braeden extended his arm and tucked hers close to his body. "What is it, lass? Ye look concerned."

"I'm afraid Alice is truly sick, not merely tired." She turned her head so the maid wouldn't hear her.

"Why do ye say so?"

"When I took her hand just now to walk with her to the shaded area, it was obvious to me she has a fever. A very high one, I'm afraid."

Braeden came to a stop and regarded her. "There are usually creeks running through the wooded areas, perhaps we can find one while we wait for the footman. Cool water on her face and neck would help the woman."

"Yes, I agree. My mother often submerged us in chilled

water when we were children to bring down fevers. Do we have something with which to carry water?"

"I keep a cup in my satchel when I travel. I'll retrieve it, and we can begin our search. I'll make sure the driver and footman stay near your maid. Why don't ye see how she is feeling? Let her know we are doing what we can to help."

Sarah headed toward Alice sitting under the trees, her eyes closed once again. As she drew nearer, the maid opened her eyes. "My lady, I fear I am not well."

"Yes, I know, Alice. You appear to have a fever. Professor McKinnon and I are going to search for a stream or creek to collect water to cool you down at bit."

"I don't wish to cause trouble, my lady."

"You are not to worry. Just stay here in the shade, and we will be back as soon as we are able. Professor McKinnon is instructing the driver and footman to stay nearby."

Alice nodded and stared blankly ahead. "Thank you."

Sarah joined Braeden, and they began to traipse through the wooded area. Dappled sunlight lit the way as they went farther into the damp forest. Sarah was careful not to step in any small animal holes as she followed Braeden. She also had to be aware of roots and branches sticking up as they walked.

Truth be told, she was anxious about going so far away from the carriage but trusted he knew what he was doing. It would seem all his intelligence should help them find something as simple as a creek.

After about ten minutes Braeden stopped. "Ah!"

"What?"

He closed his eyes and sniffed. "Water is nearby."

"How do you know?"

"Look at the vegetation surrounding us. If ye note the color and substance of…"

He waved his hands around and proceeded to provide her with a lengthy scientific explanation that soon had her eyes glazing over. The man was a wealth of information. She'd never met anyone like him in her life.

"Come this way." He hurried through the brush and she followed along. "I'm sorry to make ye stumble about in the woods like this. I thought we would find water sooner. 'Tis not a proper place for a lady." He spoke over his shoulder as he moved branches aside and held them so they wouldn't smack her.

"Nothing about this trip has been proper. It is a good thing my mother didn't believe ladies should be brought up to assume every untoward event should have them swooning all over the place. We were a different sort of family growing up."

He came to an abrupt halt, almost causing her to walk right into him. "I should like to hear about that sometime." He pointed to his right. "There."

The floor of the woods had gotten quite damp, so Sarah picked up her skirts, trying to avoid getting them muddy, although her slippers were sure to take a beating. About ten feet in front of them was a small creek, the rapidly flowing water swirling over rocks, carrying small sticks and leaves.

"I didn't realize one could locate water by the vegetation surrounding it." She watched as Braeden dipped his cup into the cool water. He drank some himself and then submerged the goblet again and held it out toward her. "Do you want a drink?"

"Yes. Actually, I am parched." She moved closer and

took the cup from his hand. Their fingers touched, and her eyes went immediately to his face. He looked back at her as if surprised. Flustered at her reaction, she took the cup and drank, closing her eyes as the cool liquid washed her mouth and slid down her throat.

She handed the cup back to Braeden, wiping her tongue over her lips.

Braeden held back a groan as the lass licked her delectable lips. Despite riding outside the carriage all afternoon, he'd been aware of her trying to read inside. He'd seen her glancing out the carriage window at him when he rode by. He'd also noticed she hadn't turned a page the entire ride so far.

It was perhaps time to admit that the lass had cast a spell over him. He wanted nothing more right now than to take the cup from her hand and draw her near. Rest his palms on her cheeks and take her mouth in a kiss of possession. Mark her as his.

The flush on her cheeks told him her thoughts were heading in the same direction. She held the cup out to him, and he reached for it, pulling her close. Her sweet mouth formed a circle, as he continued to tug until she was flat against his chest. "*Ach*, lass, 'tis something I need to do."

He admired her for not pretending she didn't know what he meant. He dropped the cup to the ground and held her face as she slid her hands up his chest to anchor on his shoulders. His head descended, and his lips covered hers. Her lips were as he imagined, sweet and full. He nibbled and licked until she opened and he swept in.

Braeden wrapped his arms around her waist and pulled her closer to the part of his body that screamed for her. If he shocked the lass, she didn't show it, instead, she fisted his jacket in her hands. The innocence in her kiss moved him as much as her taste. Following his lead, she eased her tongue into his mouth, delicately touching him.

He was certainly not an untried youth, but with his reaction to her he might as well have been. He wanted to lay her down right there on the forest floor and take her, claim her for his own. Remove her clothing and run his hands over her curves, feel the softening and dampening in her woman's parts as her body reacted to her passion.

Before he did just that, he pulled back and, panting as if he'd run a race, leaned his forehead against hers. "*Ach*, lass, what are ye doing to me?"

She gave him a slow smile, running her tongue over her dry lips. "That was nice."

"Nice?"

She pulled away and smoothed her hair back. "Yes. Nice. Very nice."

He placed his hands on his hips and shook his head. "'Twas more than just nice. If ye don't think so, I'll need to try again."

"Not now, you won't." She bent and picked up the cup he'd dropped and swept past him to reach the creek. Gathering her gown in her fist, she scooped up water and turned. "Alice needs water."

Had the lass been so unmoved by something that had almost brought him to his knees? Nay, her face was flushed and her breathing as rapid as his. For some reason she refused to acknowledge how he'd affected her. "Aye. She does need the water."

He held out his hand and she placed hers there. He grinned when the delicate little hand she placed in his shook.

Unaffected? Not bloody likely.

Alice didn't look any better and, in fact, looked worse when they returned. She took a few sips of the water from the cup, then Sarah dipped her handkerchief in the remainder and used it to pat the maid's face and the back of her neck.

Braeden paced and Sarah sat next to Alice, stroking her hand while they waited for the footman to return.

After a couple of hours, Sarah asked, "From where did you hire the footman? Will he, in fact, even return?"

"Aye. He is the innkeeper's nephew. I paid him only half of what I promised. The rest he will receive when we arrive at Bedlay Castle."

Sarah sighed. "It seems such a long time since he left."

Braeden stopped pacing and looked down the road. "I think our footman has returned."

The young man halted the horse and swung down. He untied the wheel strapped to the second horse's saddle. "The old one couldn't be fixed, so they gave me a new one."

Within minutes the four men had the new wheel on the carriage. Sarah helped Alice from the tree stump back to the carriage. Braeden worried that the maid was looking worse with every minute. "I think we better stop at the next inn. Perhaps we can find a physician to look at yer maid."

"I agree." Sarah accepted his hand and entered the carriage, sitting alongside Alice who seemed to be in a near delirium.

By the time they'd reached the Applecross Inn, Alice

appeared almost herself again. She said her fever was gone, along with whatever aches and pain she'd had. But, since it had been a long day, and nightfall was within the hour, Braeden suggested they stop for the night, anyway.

"How far behind schedule are we now?" Sarah asked as the innkeeper led them upstairs to their rooms.

"*Ach*, lass. If we had a schedule—which we dinna—we would be a day or so behind."

"My sister will be quite worried."

"Dinna fash yerself. See to getting refreshed, and we will have a bit of supper. The smells coming from the kitchen are far better than the last inn."

S arah had to agree with Braeden's comment. Because she'd eaten so little at tea time, her stomach let out with a most unladylike growl as the door to their room closed.

"My lady, if it is all right with you, I believe I will skip supper and merely rest for the remainder of the evening."

Sarah touched her fingers to Alice's forehead, which remained cool. "Are you sure? Maybe a bowl of soup would go down well?"

"No thank you. My stomach is troubling me a bit, so I'd rather not eat. I'll rest here, and when you return, you can awaken me to help you undress."

"No need to do that. I'm sure I can manage. Try to get some sleep, and I am sure you will be fine tomorrow."

Once the maid was settled under the covers, Sarah left the room to join Braeden for supper. The innkeeper's daughter directed her to a private dining room where

Braeden waited for her. One look at him and her heart took a tiny leap in her chest.

She'd tried very hard to hide her reaction to his kiss in the woods. Aside from a slight peck that Lord Manning had given her when they'd walked in the garden during his mother's house party, she'd never been kissed. Not for lack of gentlemen trying. But she'd always managed to duck just in time to avoid their lips. Somehow she knew Braeden's kiss was unlike any other she would have received.

What astounded her most was that she'd allowed it. As their hands had touched, she'd immediately known his intention. The look in his eyes, the movement toward her, all signaled his purpose. For once in her life she hadn't wanted to turn away. She had *wanted* to experience a kiss from Braeden McKinnon.

Whatever she'd expected had not been anything like the actual joining of their lips. It was gentle at first, then Braeden had become more insistent, and she'd found following his lead was quite pleasurable.

She'd once caught her sister Abigail being kissed by her husband, Joseph. Despite her decision to put off any idea of marriage for a few years, the feelings she'd experienced witnessing the passion between them had left her with a sense of loss, of missing something very important in life. After Braeden's kiss, she no longer felt left out. But what she *had* been left with frightened her a great deal.

He held out her chair and she sat, trying very hard to avoid his piercing gaze. "How is yer maid?"

"I don't actually know, for sure. She says she is only tired, but she has already slept most of the day."

"She is not having supper?"

Sarah shook her head as a young girl brought a platter of meat, a bowl of stewed vegetables, warm bread, and fresh butter and set it on the table. "May I have a pot of tea, please?"

"Yes, my lady." The girl did a quick curtsy and left the room.

Sarah picked up her fork. "Alice says she isn't hungry, merely tired."

They ate the meal in relative silence, the sound of the fire behind them crackling with a soothing sound. The food was very good, as was the tea. The long day was catching up with her.

Braeden tilted his lips in a slow smile. "Are you ready to retire, lass?"

"Yes." Sarah stifled a yawn. "I believe I am. I'd forgotten how tiring travel can be."

He stood and pulled her chair out. Extending his arm, they left the room together. She preceded him up the stairs and stopped at the door to her room. She turned to say good night, and her breath caught.

He's going to kiss me again.

Chapter Five

Braeden rested his forearm against the doorframe and leaned in. He regarded Sarah with a rakish grin. "So lass, ye think my kiss was merely 'nice'?"

She raised her chin, her eyes flashing. "Yes, truly. It was…nice."

"*Ach*, 'tis an insult to be sure, and 'tis time to change yer mind."

"I don't think…"

He cupped her face, and his mouth covered hers hungrily. All rational thought fled like water from a hole in a dam. The strength of his lips against hers went straight to her knees, turning them to liquid. If it weren't for his muscled arm that moved down to anchor tightly around her waist, there was a good chance she would slide to the floor in a crumpled heap. Just like the swooning misses she'd always viewed with disdain.

She did not want to feel the power he held over her,

tried very hard to push away the emotions racing through her. If she could, she'd command these unwanted feelings to a compartment in her brain that she would label *revisit when far away from Braeden McKinnon*. In some ways, the man was more dangerous than the highwaymen she'd feared.

Braedon released her lips and pulled back, staring at her, flashing a devilish smile. "Lass, it appears ye are having trouble standing. Do ye think ye might have contracted whatever it is yer maid has come down with?" His eyes sparkled as he added, "Aye, it must be so, since yer lovely cheeks are flushed, and ye feel warm."

She covered her cheeks with her palms. "It is merely hot in here."

He tapped the end of her nose with his index finger. "Or perhaps my kiss is not 'just nice' after all, aye?" With that he pushed himself away from the doorjamb and strolled to his room two doors down. When he reached his destination, he turned. "Good night, lass."

Sarah fought to retain her dignity as she wished him a good night as well. How effective her words were remained questionable, since her voice croaked, which brought a soft, dangerous laugh from Braeden. He left her standing in the corridor as he opened his door and stepped into the room. Before he closed it, he poked his head out. "Best to get inside and lock yer door, lass. You never know who might wish to join ye."

She scurried inside and leaned against the door, attempting to catch her breath. The only visitor she needed to concern herself with was her traveling companion. What was even more disconcerting was that if it weren't for Alice sleeping only feet from her, she might not have refused him had he asked.

After all, if she were going to become the independent woman she aspired to, couldn't she experiment a bit? She shivered at the scandalous thought.

She closed her eyes and shook her head. This would never do. The Scotsman held too much power over her. He was not like the men she'd known in London, who would stay far away simply by the looks she cast in their direction. Tomorrow she would inform the professor that it would be best for him to be on his way, and she would find another means to travel to her sister.

It had not escaped her notice that she'd earned the title "ice queen" among the gentlemen of the *ton* during her Seasons. The appellation suited her, made her feel as if she were in control of her life, not merely another young miss on the marketplace, like a horse being paraded before the crowd at Tattersalls. Eventually, she'd hoped to be considered *on the shelf* and then she could live her life the way she chose. She would write her books and lavish all her affection on her nieces and nephews.

She would not allow the tall, handsome, bespectacled Scotsman to sway her, since the time to think about a man was a few years off—if at all. Perhaps, as her publisher believed, she would become the next Jane Austen or Caroline Lamb. Although she doubted she could ever flaunt convention as Caroline was wont to do.

Moving away from the door, Sarah did her best to unfasten the back of her gown. She managed to undo the few clasps near her waist, but when it became apparent she was getting nowhere, she reluctantly approached Alice, tucked away in her cot against the wall.

"Alice," she called softly.

The maid groaned but didn't move. Sarah reached out to touch her shoulder, then gasped as she jerked her hand back. The woman was burning up with fever. "Alice," she called again as she lightly shook her. "Alice. Can you wake up?"

Alice rolled onto her back. "My lady. I feel so very sick. My stomach is rolling about, and my bones feel as though they are on fire."

In all the years of her life, it had always been her mother and various nurses who had taken care of the numerous illnesses, cuts, bruises, and other catastrophes that were a part of raising six children. Trying very hard to tamp down her rising panic, her mind raced in a myriad of different directions. But she brought herself up short when one thought resonated in her head.

Braeden.

Gathering her skirts in her fists, she raced to the door and flung it open. Within seconds she was pounding on Braeden's door.

"What?" He yanked open the door. Despite her rising panic, her eyes grew wide at his bare chest and unbuttoned breeches. Curly dark hair ran down the center of his muscular chest to disappear into his waistband. Wavy curls skimmed his forehead, and he fumbled to put his spectacles on. "What's wrong, lass?"

She licked her suddenly dry lips. "Alice. She is burning up with fever. I am worried. She seems very ill. Can we ask the innkeeper if there is a physician nearby?" Sarah wrung her hands. No person could survive such a high fever.

"Calm down, lass." He grabbed a shirt from a chair by

the door and pulled it over his head, buttoning it as he strode down the corridor to her door. "Light some candles," he said over his shoulder as he headed to Alice's bed.

Sarah fumbled with a flint until the candles were lit and a soft glow cast on the reclining figure of the maid. Her face was flushed, her eyes glassed over. Braeden put the back of his hand to her forehead. "Yes. Verra warm."

"Can we fetch a physician?" Sarah asked.

Braeden motioned her to join him by the door. "'Tis the middle of nowhere here, lass. Even if there were one about, the innkeeper would surely not summon a physician in the dark of the night for a maid."

Sarah drew in a sharp breath. "A maid is still a person!"

"I ken that. But ye ken from yer own life that certain people are designated to places in society that don't demand lofty treatment."

"Seeking a physician's assistance is hardly lofty treatment. That doesn't seem right."

"Nay. I agree, but the fact remains we need to help yer maid ourselves until daylight. Then I can ride for a physician myself."

She reluctantly nodded her agreement.

"I will draw water from the well behind the inn. Gather up as many handkerchiefs and cloths as yer able. We will have to cool her down with water."

Braeden took the pitcher and bowl from the dresser and left the room while Sarah dug through her trunk for the necessary material. She cast a worried glance at Alice as the poor woman continued to thrash about and moan.

Braeden hauled the bucket up from the well and transferred water into the pitcher. The lass's maid had not looked good at all. Aside from her high fever, she had a rash spreading up from her neck. With only candlelight, it was difficult to tell where else she had the rash.

He couldn't afford any more delays. Although he'd been warned it could take up to a month or more to receive word from the committee selecting the members of the project, he'd also been advised a decision could be made rather quickly, too. This expedition was very important to him and his work. In order to be taken seriously with his peers, he needed to prove he could contribute to a team and do it well.

Another concern was the lass's worry about the delays. With her sister awaiting her arrival while anticipating the birth of her bairn, any further interruptions in their travels would be worrisome for Sarah.

Sarah.

What was he doing taunting himself with the lass? She was an innocent young lady—sister to a duke. Not the sort of woman a man trifled with. And with him in no position now or in the near future to make the lass a respectable offer, he needed to keep far away from her.

But *ach*, how the lass set his blood to pumping. Whether she was raising her eyebrows in arrogance—common for a well-bred young lady of her station—or laughing delightedly about an amusing event, he desired her. From their first meeting he'd admired her plump lips and the womanly curves veiled by her garments. Curves that became visible when the wind plastered her gown against her.

Admittedly, even though he was still very desirous of the

lass, that need had since changed to something else. After days of travel and hours spent talking and riding together, he'd grown fascinated with the woman, Lady Sarah. She was intelligent, compassionate, loyal, and amusing. He could spend months, indeed probably years, with her, and never peel away all the layers that made up the intriguing lass.

'Twas too bad his present life did not allow for pursuing a woman. Someday he wanted to take a wife and raise bairns. But not for many years. Right now his work was too important. 'Twould be a lonely existence for a wife, to be constantly saying good-bye to her husband as he left for one expedition after another. Or worse, to drag herself and their bairns from one place to the next.

Ach, but the lass is such a temptation.

Sarah had a stack of handkerchiefs ready. She'd loosened the maid's garment and proceeded to dip the cloth in the water and wipe Alice's face, neck, and hands.

"Lass, I'm thinking I'll go for more water and perhaps ye can undo her gown a bit to cool her even more."

Sarah regarded the maid as she continued to toss on her bed, thrashing about. Glancing over her shoulder as she tried to calm the woman, Sarah said, "Yes. I will loosen her gown. And I wish to thank you, Braeden. I appreciate what you are doing."

He nodded and returned to his duties.

Eight hours later Braeden had made numerous trips back and forth to the well. The poor maid's bed was soaked, as well as her nightgown and the front of Sarah's frock. He'd tried very hard all night not to notice the curve of the lass's breasts where the damp fabric clung to her fine form. The cool water, mixed with the chilly night air, also made her nipples prominent, causing his fingers to itch to pluck at them, make them rise farther. Before he teased them with his tongue.

He'd spent those same hours thinking of mathematical equations to distract himself and stifling a groan whenever his eyes drifted toward her body. Her nearness, the scent of her light floral mix combined with her natural woman's perfume, had teased and tantalized him.

She'd spent all the time she could have been sleeping caring for her maid. All the tales he'd been privy to about English ladies faded with the dark of night. Perhaps the ones he'd met in London ballrooms were of the self-centered ilk, but this woman was like no other. 'Twas no wonder Liam MacBride had fallen in love with the lass's sister.

Love. His breath caught. No need to go near that word.

The sun cast a soft glow into the room when Sarah brushed her damp forehead with the sleeve of her gown and sat back on her heels. "I think we need to see if we can find a physician. After all these hours, she is still very hot."

"Aye. I'll see to finding one for ye. In the meantime, ye need to get some rest yourself, lass. You dinna want to be catching what yer maid has."

She slowly climbed to her feet and stretched her muscles. "What I need more than anything is a strong cup of tea and a hot bath."

"I'll see to that for ye when I rouse the innkeeper."

He found the innkeeper's wife busy in the kitchen, the aroma of bread baking already permeating the air.

"*Ach*, there is no physician that I am aware of, lad. But we have a healer who tends to the local folks. I can send my son to fetch her."

"Thank ye, ma'am. Also, Lady Sarah has requested ye send up a bath for her."

"How sick is the woman?"

"Not doing well, I'm afraid. A very high fever that Lady Sarah tried all night to bring down, to no avail. She also has a rash on her face."

The woman *tsked* as she pounded another loaf of bread dough. "I'll send the healer as soon as she comes by."

After a wash, shave, and change of clothes, Braeden sat in the private dining room waiting for Sarah to join him for breakfast. The healer had not yet arrived, and Braeden was growing concerned on how long this delay would be.

"Ah, finally, a cup of tea." Sarah entered the room, dark circles under her eyes. Such a delicate looking lass, yet she had strength absent from most other ladies. So many women in her position would have been wailing about the discomforts and delays in reaching her sister. And who else would spend the night cooling her maid down from a fever? The same lass, he assumed, who would comfort her maid after a carriage accident.

He stood and pulled out her chair. "You are looking a bit tired, lass."

"Yes. I am. But I'm more concerned now with the healer. Has she sent word yet?"

"Aye. She was attending a birth, but Mrs. Applebaum, the innkeeper's wife, said the woman would be here as soon as possible."

They shared a filling but quiet breakfast of sausage, eggs, and haggis. "Dinna care for the haggis, lass?"

She wrinkled her nose. "No. I have had it before. It is not one of my favorites."

"McKinnon! Is that you?" His old friend, Macon Campbell, filled the doorway of the dining room with his large frame. He grinned from ear to ear as he stuck out his hand and strode toward Braeden.

Braeden jumped up from his seat, a smile on his face, as he met the man halfway across the room. "Campbell, what brings ye out this way?"

"My da sent me to escort my sister home from London."

"London?"

"Yes. The lass has been staying with our aunt for a spell." Macon glanced past Braeden. "Is that yer wife? Have ye married like yer cousin and I dinna ken?"

"Nay. Come meet Lady Sarah. She's twin sister to The MacBride's new wife. I am escorting her to visit Bedlay Castle."

The two headed to the table where Sarah sat, fiddling with her teacup. A slight flush on her cheeks told him she must have heard Campbell's remark.

"Lady Sarah, this is Macon Campbell, kin to me in some way. We never did figure out how."

Campbell bowed. "My lady. 'Tis a pleasure to meet ye."

"And you as well, Mr. Campbell."

"Ah, 'tis a beauty this one, McKinnon. And a twin to The MacBride's wife?"

Sarah attempted a smile, the flush on her face growing deeper. "Yes, Mr. Campbell. Lady MacBride is my twin sister."

Sarah felt her face heat and tried desperately to calm herself. What must Mr. Campbell think of her traveling alone with Braeden? No proper lady would do such a thing. Of course, their circumstances were such at this point, with all their mishaps and Alice's illness, that there was no choice. Yet, she'd never been so embarrassed in her life. Nevertheless, Braeden didn't seem at all disturbed by them being caught alone together having breakfast. But then, men rarely had to concern themselves with such things.

"Have ye eaten breakfast?" Braeden waved Mr. Campbell to an extra chair at the table.

"Aye, I have. Right now I'm waiting for my horse to be brought around so I can continue on my way."

"My maid is sick," Sarah blurted out to no one in particular.

"Aye? Sorry to hear that, my lady."

"Yes. That is why she is upstairs right now. Not that she would be eating with us, anyway, but she is traveling with us. Just not here. Not right now..." Goodness, she was babbling like a schoolgirl caught drawing pictures by her governess instead of doing her times tables.

Braeden leaned back in his chair, crossing his arms over his chest. "Aye, we're waiting for the healer to arrive."

"Mr. Campbell, yer horse is ready." A young boy, his two front teeth missing and his cap pulled low on his forehead, grinned at the large man.

"Thank ye, lad." Mr. Campbell turned to Sarah. "I wish yer maid a quick recovery and a safe journey for all of ye, my lady."

Slapping Braeden on his back, Campbell strolled with Braeden to the door, leaving Sarah alone with her thoughts. Up until now she really hadn't given much thought to the impropriety of her traveling with Braeden. Alice, of course, had been with her to lend some respectability to the trip, but she was definitely treading in dangerous waters here if word got back to England.

She would be ruined!

She dismissed the thought, realizing whomever they would meet along the way would most likely not know her or any of her family members. She was getting herself all worked up for no cause.

"Sarah, the healer is upstairs now with Alice." Braeden stuck his head in the door.

"Thank you." Shoving aside the dilemma in which she found herself, she followed him up the stairs to her bedchamber and eased the door open.

A stout woman with fiery red hair tucked somewhat under a white cap leaned over Alice's bed, examining her face. She ran stubby fingers over the rash that had appeared during the night. "Typhus."

"Excuse me?" Sarah said, approaching the bed.

"The lass has typhus. I've seen it many times before."

Afraid of having Alice hear the healer's comments, Sarah took the woman by the elbow and brought her to the door where Braeden waited. "Is this something very contagious?"

"Nay. I dinna think so. I've seen many a mum take care of little ones with the disease and not catch it herself. There's thinking that it comes from a bug bite of some sort."

Sarah shuddered, wondering how in heaven's name Alice would have picked up this disease. "What type of treatment do you recommend?"

The woman rolled her sleeves to her elbows and fisted her hands on her hips. "If ye had a physician here, he'd be telling ye to have her blood let, but not Maggie. No, lass, Maggie does not bleed her patients." She nodded vigorously.

Since Sarah assumed *Maggie* was the healer standing in front of her, she was grateful about the bloodletting as she had never understood how that could be beneficial to a patient. "Then what do you suggest?"

"I will make a tisane for the lass. She must drink it five times a day. Keep the windows closed and the room warm, so she can sweat out the fever."

"When will she be able to travel?"

The healer glanced back over at Alice and shook her head. "*Ach*, lass. She won't be able to travel for two or three weeks."

"Two or three weeks!" Braeden and Sarah said at the same time.

Chapter Six

"We cannot possibly wait another two or three weeks," Sarah said. "My sister is expecting me, and by now she must be very concerned. That is not good for her and the babe."

"Aye. We could send a message to relieve her mind."

Sarah continued to pace and wring her hands. "Yes, I will do that, which will ease her mind, but this is a disaster. I don't want to wait two or three weeks. What are we to do?"

Braeden sat with his long legs stretched out, his feet crossed at the ankles. He studied his boots and attempted to work up enough nerve to state his case to the lass. He also could not languish in this place. His letter and the expedition awaited him.

"Sarah, sit down. Ye are wearing out the boards."

She sat at the very edge of the chair, her hands in her lap, the only indication of her disquiet the tiny slipper peeking out from her dress that tapped a cadence on the floor. "I am sitting. Now we must rationally discuss this dilemma."

Braeden stood and took her spot as he paced, running his fingers through his hair. "We have to be practical, lass."

"Yes."

"As much as it pains me to say this, we must leave yer maid here under the care of the healer."

Sarah continued to stare at him, chewing her lip. "I agree."

Braeden let out a sigh of relief.

"But…"

He sucked the air back in.

"I cannot travel alone with you." Her shoulders slumped. "It is not proper."

If the lass only knew how very improper his thoughts had been almost since the time they'd met, she would surely run screaming from the room. The problem of them being alone together on the road for a few more days had troubled him when he'd made his suggestion. But he would have to be strong and fight this attraction he felt for the lass.

"The only other solution is for me to ride on ahead and stop at Bedlay Castle and tell yer sister where ye are. Then Liam can send back a carriage for ye."

Sarah's eyes grew wide. "Being alone at a public inn with no male protection is even worse than us traveling together."

"Aye. 'Tis true, that."

After a few minutes, Sarah brightened. "I can wear breeches and a shirt and we can travel on horses as brothers. I can have my trunks sent on with Alice when she recovers. It will be even faster that way."

Braeden gasped and began coughing, his previous improper thoughts turning downright indecent at the lass's suggestion. Subjecting himself to days of watching her charming backside and legs outlined in breeches had him aching in the wrong spot. No matter how much the lass would try to disguise herself, her being taken for a boy gave "farfetched" a new definition.

It appeared every solution they came up with was worse than the one before. "Nay, lass. I dinna think ye would be taken for a lad."

She straightened her shoulders. "I dress in breeches all the time when I'm riding in the country."

More indecent pictures flitted through his mind. Braeden held up his hand, desperately wanting to eliminate that vision. "But I doubt yer trying to pass yerself off as a lad at yer own home. Nay. It won't work."

"Then what shall we do?" She continued to chew that temptingly full lip, only reinforcing the desire that tightened his muscles. He had to get his lustful wanderings to behave themselves.

"We can try to hire ye a maid from the town."

She shook her head. "No. By the time we interviewed candidates and found someone acceptable, Alice will be recovered."

The lass was smart, no doubt about that. He'd been so busy ogling her and thinking about them being alone for days with no chaperone that his normally sharp mind was withering fast. They had to get this resolved, on the road, and her in the safe hands of her sister. "What are the chances that someone who knows ye will also be traveling to the Highlands of Scotland?"

"I doubt any of the *ton* would be caught dead here."

Braeden scowled at the insult to his beloved land. "'Twas not a nice thing to say, lass."

"I'm sorry, truly. I didn't mean it the way it sounded." She twisted her fingers, her disquiet evident in her movements. "I'm not thinking clearly. But I do sincerely believe there is no chance I would meet anyone of my acquaintance."

"Then we have nothing with which to concern ourselves. From here 'tis a three day trip, and then ye will be within the safety of yer family."

And far away from him and his lusty thoughts.

She tapped her finger on her chin, a slight smile gracing her lovely face. "I suppose you are correct." After a few more minutes of consideration, she nodded. "Yes. I think that is the best solution. I will make arrangements for someone to see to Alice while she is recovering, and assure her that once I arrive at Bedlay Castle I will send a carriage back for her."

Braeden rubbed his hands together. "Excellent. We can put many miles on the road today."

He pushed to the back of his mind the idea that kept nudging at him. Hours spent in the lass's company with no chaperone. While the tenets of the *ton* meant nothing to him, he knew enough about Polite Society to understand Sarah would be in grave danger of ruination if word of this trip trickled back to London. Or her brother. He broke into a sweat at the thought of a duke coming after him for ruining his sister.

They would be forced to marry. Aside from the problem that would arise from his work, the idea was not a totally unpleasant one. In fact, not an unpleasant one at all.

Best to get that one out of yer foolish head, McKinnon.

S arah gave Alice one more hug and assured her in about a week's time the carriage would return for her and wait until she was ready to travel.

"I am so sorry for the trouble I've caused you, my lady." The maid wiped the tears running down her cheeks.

"Don't worry about it. All will be fine."

"But you're traveling alone with the professor. Your brother would have my head if he knew I'd allowed you to continue on this journey without me."

"You need not worry about that." Despite her own concerns about the trip alone with Braeden, Sarah smoothed back the hair from Alice's forehead. "Drake will never know, and in a few days I will be with Sybil. Why, by now she might even have already had her babe."

Sarah rose and left the room, closing the door softly. Taking a deep breath, she joined Braeden downstairs. One thing Alice was correct about. Should Drake discover she traveled, by herself, with a man whom she'd only met on the road a few days ago, he would surely lock her in her room for the remainder of her days. Or send her off to a convent.

"Are ye ready, lass?" Braeden stood at the door, tall, imposing, and sinfully handsome. His tight breeches outlined every muscle in his well-developed thighs above shining Hessian boots. His snug dark blue jacket exhibited broad shoulders for which no tailor had to add padding. A wicked smile beneath mirthful blue eyes had her heart pumping as he held out his arm for her to take. She licked her dry lips and moved forward as if going to her doom.

I am in so much trouble.

The cool spring morning air refreshed her, body and soul, after hours in a sick room. Sarah inhaled the pleasant smell of leaves and foliage dampened by two days of rain. Bright sunlight reflected off the carriage, raising her spirits even further. In just a few days she would see her beloved twin again. And possibly her new niece or nephew. She was foolish to worry. Everything would be just fine.

"What do you mean we won't make as many miles today as we planned?" Sarah stood outside the carriage door, her hands on her hips. They'd just finished their tea at a lovely inn, and she was ready to ride another five or six hours to get closer to Sybil.

"The stable only had two fresh horses, so we won't be able to travel very fast, or we will wear them out altogether and be left on the side of the road."

She walked in a tight circle staring at the ground at this latest delay. Only two horses pulling the carriage would make for a much slower pace. But it was still better than waiting here for more horses to show up and be made ready.

"I will continue to ride Niels to lighten the load, but we still won't go as far as we could have with four horses."

Grumbling under her breath, Sarah climbed into the carriage with Braeden's assistance. "Dinna talk under yer breath lass, 'tis not proper."

She gritted her teeth. Braeden had been teasing her all morning about what was, and was not, proper. He might think this was all a joke, but if word traveled back to London about this trip, her reputation would be in shreds.

Then I wouldn't have to worry about being pressured into marriage.

Except, it could ruin her sister Mary's chances of a decent match. Although, when she'd left home, an American, Mr. Marcus Pensworth, had been paying Mary a bit of attention.

The morning passed rather quickly. Once they returned to the carriage after luncheon, Sarah slid her manuscript out from her satchel and leaned back, prepared to read. The rocking of the carriage, the meal she'd consumed, and the lack of sleep the previous night took its toll, however, and soon she was being shaken awake. "Lass, we're at our stop."

She blinked and stared directly into a pair of now familiar sharp blue eyes. Her heart began to thump and she licked her lips. How long had he been watching her sleep? Had her mouth hung open? Was she drooling? Oh Lord, why did he keep staring at her with that teasing smile on his lips?

"Come along, lass. I am ready for my dinner. 'Tis been a long day." He held out his hand and helped her from the carriage.

The Beresford Inn was a lively place with raucous laughter coming from within, which grew even louder as the door swung open to allow two men to leave. Once they made their way through the throng they stopped at the bar where the man behind it shoved one tankard of beer after another to the men lining the area.

"Can I help ye, lad?" The bartender wiped his hands on a large apron surrounding his corpulent middle.

"Yes. The lady and I would like dinner. Do ye have a private dining room?"

"Nay. We had so many patrons tonight we had to open it for everyone. 'Tis cockfight night, always a crowd. I can get ye a seat, though. Will ye be needin' a room?"

"Two rooms." Braeden held up two fingers. "And I need fresh horses for the morning. Do ye have a stable?"

"Aye. I can fix ye up. Let me get my wife to help the lady."

"Thank you." Braeden took Sarah by the elbow and maneuvered her around the crowd to a quieter area near a fireplace. "'Tis sorry I am about the place. But I don't think our horses will make it to the next inn."

"A cockfight?"

"Aye, a few inns along the way hold them for the towns-people's entertainment."

"That's terrible."

"For the cocks, I imagine. The men seem to enjoy it."

She would never understand men. To stand around and watch two roosters fight each other to the death was ridiculous. Men had the most peculiar interests. A question jumped into her head. "Do you like cockfights?"

"Nay. I think it a barbarous sport. If I'm to see an animal killed 'twill be for my dinner. But I wouldn't say too much about it here, lass." He gestured toward a group of heavily drinking men shouting at each other. "The men seem quite ready for the game. In case yer interested, the sport is a couple hundred years old. The book *The Commendation of Cocks and Cock Fighting* was published in 1607. However, during Magellan's voyage of discovery of the Philippines in 1521 he witnessed cockfighting. 'Twas documented by Antonio Pigafetta."

She gaped at him. "You have all this information stored somewhere up there in your brain?"

He shrugged and cast her a boyish smile. Another point for Braeden McKinnon. Not that she was keeping score, of course. It just interested her how civilized, intelligent, and respectable the man was.

Anxious to get her mind off her traveling companion, she said, "I find I am still tired, so I will be happy to have dinner and retire to my room. Perhaps we can start out earlier tomorrow to make up for the shortened day today?"

"I will tell the innkeeper to have the horses ready at dawn."

"Good evening, my lady. Mr. McClune tells me ye want two rooms?" The innkeeper's wife regarded them with raised eyebrows, and Sarah immediately felt the disapproval in the woman's eyes. Here she was being judged by a tradeswoman for traveling alone with a man who obviously wasn't her husband, or they would be sharing a room.

Sarah nodded. "Yes, please. We had to leave my maid behind at the last inn. She was suffering an illness and couldn't travel." Now why in heaven's name did she feel the need to explain herself to a serving woman?

She looked helplessly at Braeden who didn't seem the least bit concerned. She had an inane desire to kick him in the shins.

"Well, if you will follow me, my lady, I can get ye settled upstairs in yer room." The innkeeper's wife started up the stairs, then spoke over her shoulder to Braeden. "We have a room on this floor where ye can sleep."

Sarah almost laughed out loud at the woman's statement. Apparently Mrs. McClune was not going to countenance any shenanigans under her nose.

The inn had quieted by the time they had refreshed themselves and were settled at a lovely table near the fireplace. Raucous shouts from behind the inn could be heard, but Sarah blocked them out. Mrs. McClune brought them a basket of warm, fragrant bread, a crock of butter, and two bowls of the most wonderful lamb stew Sarah had ever tasted.

Delicious food and the two glasses of wine she'd consumed had her more than ready to seek her bed. The little bit of a nap she'd received that afternoon had helped, but still she felt tired to her bones.

"I'll see ye to yer room, lass." Braeden stood and held his hand out. "Ye look like yer about to fall asleep in yer tea."

"Yes, that is quite true." She took hold of his hand, and they walked upstairs. Sarah glanced around as they made their way from the table to the staircase, afraid Mrs. McClune would jump out from behind a door and shout "aha!" at them.

She comforted herself with the fact that they only had another two, maybe three, nights before they would reach Bedlay Castle. There she would be safe from the man walking behind her and the feelings he coaxed from her untried body. She needed to stop being so aware of Braeden. The warmth from his closeness reached her back, making her shiver with expectation. Of what, she was afraid to consider.

Once they arrived at her door, she opened it quickly. "Good night."

"Wait a minute, lass," Braeden said, closing it softly and tugging her to him. "I'm not happy with ye being up here with myself downstairs. I think the innkeeper wanted to protect yer virtue, but in the meantime might have put ye in danger. Be sure to lock that door and shove a chair underneath the latch."

Her heart thumped at his words. She'd been so focused on his nearness all through dinner and the walk upstairs, she hadn't thought about the risks of her being on a different floor all night. "I agree. I think Mrs. McClune thought to guard my reputation, when in fact she made things a bit precarious for me."

"Aye. I've thought of nothing else since we arrived." He paused, then added, "I could come inside and sleep on the floor."

There was no teasing in his voice or mannerism, and she might have seriously considered it if she hadn't already been subjected to his kisses. The temptation was too strong and his nearness too heady. The innkeeper certainly knew what she was about. "I am sure all will be fine. As you say, I will lock the door and block it with a chair. Also, I have strong lungs. If someone were to attempt to enter, you will be able to hear me in the next town."

"Aye, lass. Use that fine strong voice of yers if ye need me." He lazily tucked the hair behind her ear that had fallen from her bun. "Whatever way you might need me."

Heat rose to her face at his suggestion—not at all as innocent as he pretended it to be. Why did he affect her so, when she had been quite able to handle the men who'd attempted to court her in London? There, no one had caught her fancy. Even if she had been tempted to allow a man to court her, none had presented himself who made her feel the way Braeden did.

She studied his face as she realized it was a quirk of fate that the one man who could tempt her to forget her pledge not to marry for a long time, if at all, in order to concentrate on her career as an author, had ended up alone with her—far, far from home and the judgmental eyes of the *ton*.

Nonsense. This trip would be over shortly, Braeden

would leave her with Sybil, and be on his way to this expedition he was so anxious to join. Then she would come to know her new niece or nephew while she awaited word from her publisher on the release of her book. Once again the anticipation rose as she considered how surprised her family would be when her book appeared on the local bookstore shelves.

"What has ye so thoughtful?" He ran his knuckle down her cheek.

"I am concerned about my sister and how anxious she must be for me to arrive," she lied.

"*Ach*, lass. 'Twas not what ye were thinking. Yer mouth says one thing, but yer eyes another." Now he was twisting one of her curls around his finger. "Perhaps ye were thinking the same thing I am."

"N-no, I don't believe so."

"Are ye sure?" He leaned in closer, the faint scent of the wine he'd drunk wafting over her. "I believe ye are thinking about kissing me and how much ye enjoyed it the last time."

She shook her head furiously. He anchored it with his hands, and his head descended, taking her lips in complete possession, asking for surrender, and allowing nothing less. His tongue swept into her mouth, encouraging her to join him in a lovers' dance. Her previous dark thoughts fled as she gave him all that he demanded and more, enjoying the warmth and moistness of his caress.

By the time he drew back and rested his forehead on hers, she wasn't quite sure where she stood and if her legs would even hold her. She clung to his shoulders, relying on the strong grasp of his arm around her waist to keep her from tumbling to the floor in a passionate stupor. How many times would he put her into this state before she wanted more, knowing there was much more to be had?

"Ye have me under a spell, Lady Sarah." His eyes roamed her face, searching for what he wanted and what, she was afraid, he would see. Could he sense how close she was to surrender? How near she was at this moment to yielding to the one thing that would change her forever, and might even rip her away from her well-planned life?

A life with a chance to be the woman she wanted to be, without the burden of a husband?

Chapter Seven

After a fitful night's sleep on a cot too small for him, Braeden sat on the edge of the bed and ran his fingers through his hair, trying very hard to wake up. He fumbled with a flint in the darkness and lit a candle. He'd been up and down the stairs all night, checking on Sarah, making sure none of the boisterous men who'd made their way back to the inn after the cockfight caused trouble.

In the dimness of his room he was able to have a quick wash and dress himself. The innkeeper was already cleaning up from the prior night's gaiety, and the smell of cinnamon buns coming from the kitchen signaled that Mrs. McClune was busy as well.

"Good mornin' to ye, Mr. McKinnon," the innkeeper said. "Are ye and the lady leaving early, then?"

"Aye. Are the horses ready?"

"I sent my lad to the stable a bit ago. By the time ye and yer lady friend have broken yer fast, he'll have them hitched to yer carriage."

"Thank you. I will just go wake Lady Sarah."

"Nay." The innkeeper stopped sweeping and glowered at him. "I will send my wife to help the lady. She attended to her last night."

"Of course. I forgot she would need assistance. I dinna think of her dressing. I mean, that she would need help in dressing. But then," he hurried on, "I'm not familiar with her dressing at all…" He tugged at his neckcloth, then waved in the direction of the private dining room. "I will just wait for her down here, then."

By the saints! He was blathering like a lad caught with his hand in the milking maid's bodice. 'Twas almost as if the innkeeper and his wife knew Braeden's lecherous thoughts.

Within minutes of settling into a chair in front of the fireplace in the private dining room, Braden caught a glimpse of Mrs. McClune hurrying past the door and up the stairs. Would this blasted trip never be over? Had he not run into Lady Sarah and her maid on the side of the road, he'd be home by now, with his much anticipated letter already in hand.

But then he would never have met the woman who was causing him a distraction of immense proportions. His brain hadn't been this befuddled since he'd been a dissolute youth during his later student years at university. He needed to get home so he could focus on his work. Not spend his time thinking improper thoughts about a very proper lady. The sister of a duke, he reminded himself. A duke who most likely owned a pistol. Indeed, probably several of them.

A young girl brought him a pot of tea. She gave him a slight smile and curtsied. "Did ye be wantin' your breakfast now, or are ye waitin' for yer lady?"

"I'll wait, thank you." As he sipped the bracing liquid it occurred to him that perhaps he and Sarah had not thought this out completely. With the way Mrs. McClune had regarded him, their traveling together could pose quite a problem for Sarah. He would have to come up with an idea to protect her reputation for the rest of the trip.

Sarah packed the last of her few items into her satchel and left the room. She didn't know whether to laugh or cry at the "lecture" she'd gotten from Mrs. McClune. It was obvious the innkeeper's wife thought it a disgrace that she was a young unmarried lady traveling alone with a man not a relative. Even Sarah's explanation of Alice's illness had held no sway with the woman. She was of the opinion that a woman's reputation was worth whatever inconvenience she needed to suffer.

The innkeeper's wife managed to increase Sarah's guilt and sense of unease. She was very thoughtful as she descended the stairs to the main room. The inn was very quiet, with just a few men drinking ale, unlike when she had tried to sleep last night. She shuddered at the idea of ale in the morning.

Braeden sat at a small table in the private dining room, also deep in thought. "Good morning," she said as she slid into a seat across from him.

"Good morning, lass. I don't think there's any point in asking if ye slept well, because the cockfight went on for quite some time, and the celebration even longer."

"True. I must admit I was a bit nervous with the men in

and out of the inn all night."

"Aye. If it makes ye feel any better now, I took a few trips up and down the stairs until the wee hours to make sure no one attempted to keep ye company."

"Ah. That must be why Mrs. McClune thought to reprove me this morning." Sarah poured tea into her cup. "She spent a good deal of time warning me about the dangers in the world for a young lady without proper protection, and how easily they can be 'fooled' as she put it, into doing something of which their mothers would not approve."

"*Ach*. The woman gave me a few curt responses and unfriendly looks this morning. She must have heard me going up and down and assumed it was for nefarious reasons."

A slight fluttering in Sarah's lower parts reminded her of the kisses she and Braeden had shared and what nefarious behavior could have followed. She remembered once again the book she and Sybil had snuck from Drake's room when he'd been away at school. The naughty drawings had given them lively conversations for years.

"Sarah, I'm thinking it might be best for the rest of the trip to tell people that we are brother and sister, and I am escorting you to Scotland for a visit."

"Why, Braeden, that's a wonderful idea. I wish we had thought of it yesterday."

"Well, no matter. That's how we will go on."

"However, there is just one problem."

At his raised eyebrows, she continued, "You speak with a Scottish accent and I speak with an English one."

"Aye, 'tis true. We'll have to be half brother and sister. You raised in England, me in Scotland."

She grinned at him. "*Oh, what a tangled web we weave*:

When first we practice to deceive!"

"Sir Walter Scott," Braeden offered.

She frowned. "I thought Shakespeare said that?"

"Aye, a lot of people do. But 'twasn't him."

A young girl entered the room, holding a platter of eggs, sausages, the ever present black pudding, and haggis. She placed them on the table and touched the teapot. "I will bring ye hot tea."

"Thank you," Braeden said.

They remained silent as they ate breakfast. Sarah imagined this is what it would be like if they were married. To each other. Sitting together first thing in the morning, sharing breakfast, drinking tea. Except they would have spent time in the same bed. She squirmed, again feeling that flutter in her lady parts.

"Are ye all right, lass?"

Why did she think the grin on his face resulted from him discerning her thoughts? Did he know her that well? "I'm fine. Just anxious to be on our way. I'm concerned the message we asked the innkeeper at the last stop to deliver to my sister might not have been sent."

"Aye, I'm worried about that myself. The man didn't seem too eager to have his son take the trip. The best we can do is push on." He shoved himself away from the table and pulled out Sarah's chair. The young girl came from the kitchen with a teapot in her hand. "Are ye leaving, then?"

"Yes. I'm sorry, but we are somewhat behind our schedule. Please forgive us." Sarah gave the girl a warm smile.

The young girl stared at Sarah openmouthed, as if she'd never heard an apology from a lady before. A sad thing, to her way of thinking.

After three hours on the road, Sarah found herself nodding off. Two nights of scant sleep were taking their toll. Braeden had been riding outside the coach all morning, raising her awareness of him every time he rode past the window, blocking the negligible sun. She really should make herself look away so as not to view his tight backside. But the temptation proved too great, and soon she was merely watching him, the notes she was making on her manuscript forgotten.

Her eyes had just drifted closed when they were jerked open as the carriage jolted, and she was tossed to the floor. Heavens, were they having another problem with the wheels? As she scrambled up from the floor, the sound of shouting and, *dear God*, a pistol discharging, set her heart to pounding.

Her arms extended, she braced herself as the carriage came to a screeching halt. Sarah huddled in the corner of the vehicle, trying to appear as small as possible. She tugged off the ring she'd inherited from her grandmother and shoved it quickly into her bodice. Before she had a chance to get her breathing under control the door of the vehicle flew open.

A wiry man dressed in black trousers, a black shirt and jacket, and holding a very scary pistol pointed in her direction motioned with his head. A second pistol was tucked into his trousers. "Out."

She climbed down the steps on shaky legs. The driver and two footmen sat on the ground, their hands underneath them. A second highwayman pointed a pistol at the three men. Braeden remained on his horse, his lips tightened as he watched the first man reach out and touch her hair. She instinctively pulled her head back.

"Aye, a bonny lass, this one."

"Don't touch her," Braeden growled.

"*Ach*, and what do ye think ye can do about it?" He grinned, revealing missing teeth as he pointed the pistol at Braeden. "'Tis yer lucky day, lad. All we want is yer coin, ye can keep yer wife for yerself. Lasses are too much trouble, anyway." His grin faded, his steely eyes narrowing. "Hand it over, lad. All yer coin."

"My coin is in my pocket. I canna reach it from here." Without waiting for the highwayman's permission, Braeden swung his leg over the horse, kicking the robber in the face as he came down. With very few movements, he sliced his hand through the air and knocked the pistol from the man's grip. The weapon skidded away as the man rushed him, and with a grunt, they both landed in the dirt.

Taken by surprise, the second gunman swung around, aiming his pistol at the two grappling on the ground, but with the confusion, he hesitated to fire.

"Grab the pistol," Braeden shouted in the direction of the three men. Sarah raced to where the weapon lay on the ground and picked it up. With the second highwayman distracted, the driver hopped up and grabbed a rock. With a swift movement, he smacked the second outlaw over the head. The man's knees buckled, and he collapsed to the ground.

Braeden had the first bandit facedown on the ground, his knee pressing the man's back. Panting, he glanced at Sarah. "*Ach*, lass. Be careful with that. Ye dinna want to shoot the wrong person."

She raised her chin and pressed the pistol against her skirts. "I could shoot if I had reason enough."

"Ye could?" He grinned. "A new surprise from ye every day." He flipped the highwayman onto his back and planted him a facer that knocked him unconscious. Slipping a pistol from the man's trousers, Braeden stood and glared at the footmen, as the driver, who still held the rock in his hand, gazed at the unconscious highwayman with blood dripping from his head. "Do ye think ye can come up with some cord to tie the man if ye dinna find it too much trouble?"

The two footmen scrambled to their feet. "Aye."

"Good, then get them secured, and we'll be on our way. We can leave them at the next inn for the magistrate to deal with." When they continued to stare at the man, he added, "Now!"

Braeden collected the weapon from the bandit's waist as well as the one from the man bleeding on the ground. He then sauntered to Sarah, his hand outstretched. "I'll take the pistol now, lass." He glanced to her shaky hand that held the pistol. Reaching out slowly, he eased the weapon from her grip and shoved it into the band of his breeches. "Are ye all right?"

She nodded, her mouth suddenly dry and black dots dancing in front of her eyes. Braeden rested his hand on her shoulders and pushed her gently down. "Lower yer head, lass, before ye faint."

"I don't faint," she whispered.

Oh God. Could anything else happen on this trip? Once she arrived at Sybil's home she would not leave it for years. Perhaps she would still be there when the new babe set off for university. She giggled at the idea of her growing into an aged woman under the hospitality of Laird MacBride.

Braeden rubbed circles on her back, murmuring words

she didn't understand. Gaelic, most likely, since she spoke three languages, but Gaelic was not among them. Suddenly the tears welled in her eyes, and her body began to shake. Braeden scooped her up and strode to the carriage. He climbed in and settled her on his lap where she proceeded to weep for the disaster this journey had become.

"'Tis all right, lass. 'Tis over now. Ye are safe."

She shoved at his chest. "Safe for now! Do you know how awful this trip has been? She counted off on her fingers. "A wrecked carriage, servants killed, Alice struck with typhus, broken wheels, rowdy inns, and now highwaymen."

"Aye, lass. 'Tis true. 'Tis been a sorry journey for ye. But ye canna fall apart on me now."

She wiped her nose with the handkerchief he handed her and sniffled. "Indeed? Then can you give me a time and place where I can fall apart?"

He tucked her loose curl behind her ear. "*Ach*, lass, I love yer sense of humor."

She cast him a slight smile. "Suppose I am not joking?"

"Then let's say ye can cry on yer sister's shoulder for days once we get ye to Bedlay. Does that suit?"

"Yes. And once I arrive, I might never leave again."

"Sir, the men are tied up. Where shall we put them?" The younger footman approached the carriage.

Sarah drew in a deep breath. "Not in here!"

"Nay, lass. Dinna fash yerself. I'll put them in here, and you will ride with me to the next posting inn." Braeden plopped her on the seat across from them and climbed out of the carriage. Sarah attempted to right herself and regain her dignity as she listened to Braeden give orders to the footmen.

How had a stuffy university professor ever gained the ability to take down a highwayman while the men they'd hired to escort them stood motionless, ready to hand over everything to the robbers? None of her preconceived notions about Braeden McKinnon had come to pass. Which was precisely why she couldn't dismiss the man as merely an escort to her sister's home.

She felt as safe with him as she did with her brother. Drake had always looked out for his mother and sisters, taking over the task from their father the day the man had been thrown from his horse and killed by a broken neck.

Braeden escorted her from the carriage and, after supervising the loading of the highwaymen, said, "Ye can sit across my lap, or ride astride like ye said ye did at yer family's country home."

Neither choice seemed appropriate. Repeating the ride they'd taken when he'd first rescued her, when her bottom had sat snug against his manhood, did not seem the wise choice.

Sarah glanced down at herself. "Since I wear my breeches when I ride astride, I don't think that's how I prefer to travel now."

Braeden nodded and scooped her up, holding her in his arms as he stepped into the stirrup and swung his leg over the horse, settling them both, her body draped across his lap. The man handled her as if she weighed nothing. How in heaven's name did someone who spent his time in front of a classroom have such strength?

Given the chance to study his features unabashed as they rode ahead of the carriage, she understood the attraction she was having such a difficult time fighting.

Strong features, chiseled chin, warm eyes behind spectacles, and hair that refused to stay off his forehead, making her fingers itch to smooth it back. She rested against his solid chest, his heart beating in her ear. The cool air rushed past them as she felt his muscled thighs under her bottom. Secure in his arms, she pondered how a genius university professor had the body of a field worker.

"Are ye having fun admiring me, lass?" He looked down at her and grinned. "Do ye see anything ye like?"

Caught like a child with her hand snatching a biscuit from Cook, she blushed until she thought her face would catch fire. She raised her chin and sniffed. "I have no idea what you mean. I was merely watching the scenery."

"Aye. 'Tis lovely scenery, for sure. All these trees, one after another. I can see why ye'd want to stare at it. Fascinating." He winked at her, and lips pursed, Sarah turned slightly so she couldn't see his face, hoping the wind would cool her heated cheeks.

They rode in silence for another hour or so while Sarah fought sleep with her comfortable position tucked against Braeden's warm body. Her head dipped occasionally, but she managed to shift herself upright. The last thing she wanted to do was curl up against him and fall asleep with the scent of his soap lulling her into slumber.

Braeden slowed the horse to a trot as the next inn came into view. Once they stopped, he jumped from the horse and reached for her. As she slid down his body, she drew in a sharp breath. Stiff from riding, she grabbed his arm as they made their way into the establishment. "Don't forget we are sister and brother."

Chapter Eight

Sarah was surprised by the number of elegant carriages in front of the inn. She certainly hadn't expected to see so many fine coaches on this road, here in the middle of the Highlands.

She dragged her feet as they entered the bustling room. The trip thus far had her muddleheaded. All she could think of was a hot bath, warm food, and a soft bed.

"Why don't you secure us two rooms while I notify the stable lad that the carriage arriving behind us contains two bandits?" Braeden spoke above the din of the crowd as he led Sarah to the innkeeper's desk.

Chaos reigned all around them. The stylish carriages had deposited more than a dozen people at the inn, all of them demanding and shouting to be heard above the others. All of them requiring special attention.

"Oh, dear. What is this about?" Sarah asked, stifling a yawn.

"I dinna ken, but I hope it doesn't mean we canna get a room."

"Two rooms."

"Aye. With the way things look, I will be happy if we dinna have to sleep in the stables."

The innkeeper was away from his post, so Sarah waited, her eyes burning from fatigue as Braeden left her to take care of notifying the stable hands. A burly man bounded down the stairs and greeted the first person in the line. The queue moved forward, with the innkeeper bowing and scraping, ordering women who must have been his family members to bring baths, prepare tea, and make note of special requests for dinner.

"Two rooms, please," Sarah said as an older woman with her maid stepped aside to follow a young girl up the stairs, complaining loudly all the way, and nudging the maid with her elbow.

"'Tis sorry I am, my lady, but I only have one room left."

Sarah chewed her lip for a moment. As tired as she was, and with the carriage still on the road with the bandits in it, she had no choice. It was perfectly acceptable for brother and sister to share a room. She and Braeden could work out the sleeping arrangements later. "That is fine, we'll take one room."

As the man fumbled for the key, Braeden walked up to the counter and touched Sarah on her arm. "'Tis taken care of."

"Professor!" The innkeeper grinned as he addressed a startled Braeden. "I dinna ken this room was for ye and yer wife."

Sarah gaped at the man. *Wife?* Her tired brain did some

fast scheming. If the innkeeper knew Braeden, chances were he also knew his sisters, and she was certainly not one of them. She could take the room herself, but then everyone within shouting distance would know she had intended to share a room with Braeden. Not good.

Pasting on a smile, she turned to Braeden. "Yes, dear, they only have one room left, so aren't we fortunate?" She tucked her arm into his and smiled at the innkeeper. "My husband and I are grateful we were able to secure the last room."

Braeden stared openmouthed and then bent to speak into her ear. "Lass, do ye realize what ye've done? Ye just told the man we're married."

"I know that, dear." She kicked him on his leg. "I told him that because we *are* married." She cast a smile at the innkeeper. "Men can be so trying at times."

B raeden didn't know whether to laugh or wail. The lass had just married them. She obviously either dinna ken, or had forgotten, that in Scotland a declaration of marriage before a witness was a legal binding of the couple. Moreover, if they spent the night together in the same room it would be considered consummation, and there would be no turning back.

He couldn't even contradict the lass. It would embarrass her, no doubt, and there were still quite a few people in the common room who had heard their exchange. Since she'd assured the innkeeper they were married, if he denied it that could be a worse scandal for the poor woman. Everyone within earshot would be certain to determine who the young lady was who tried to pass herself off as married in order to share a room with a man. He groaned inwardly at the conundrum she'd just created for them.

As they waited for another daughter to escort them to their room, he studied his newly acquired wife and wondered why he wasn't more upset by this turn of events. Of course they could get out of it by simply ignoring the whole thing once they left the inn tomorrow morning. After all, who would know what the lass had done except them?

And the innkeeper.

And the innkeeper's family.

And all the people milling about in the room whom he hadn't gotten a good look at. There was a chance he knew some of them.

But the more important question was, did he want to ignore the unexpected marriage? Sarah would be a fine wife. Beautiful, intelligent, compassionate, and best of all, spirited enough to certainly keep him content in the bedchamber.

When he'd been hired by the university, he'd put off searching for a wife. He was young, much younger than his peers, and his work came first. But there was no reason, now that it had happened, that he couldn't make it work out. A wife could certainly, if not help, at least support him in his profession.

"Braedon McKinnon, are ye here for the Quigley lass's wedding?" An unexpected slap on his back almost knocked Braedon off his feet. He turned to Donald Munro, brother to one of the lasses who had married a McKinnon lad a few years back.

"Donald. 'Tis nice to see ye." He put out his hand and

the men shook. "Nay. I'm on my way home from university and stopped here for the night," he answered. "It appears I didn't pick the best day to do it."

"Ye have the right of it, lad. The horde of us are traveling together for the wedding in Reay come this Friday." Munro looked around. "Did I see ye come in with a lass?"

Before Braeden could form an answer, the innkeeper said, "Mr. McKinnon, my daughter just took yer wife upstairs to yer room. 'Tis the third door on the left when yer ready, sir."

"Wife?" Munro asked with raised eyebrows. "So one of the lasses with her eye on ye finally caught ye, aye?"

"Aye." Braeden grinned. If only the man knew how effectively Sarah had indeed caught him. And herself.

"I'm on my way to dinner. Perhaps we can raise a toast to yer wife later?"

"Aye." He might as well drink to the occasion. Then as he watched Munro walk away to join his friends, he thought it would be best to keep Sarah's mistake from her for a while. Given what he knew of her reluctance to marry, the lass might not take it well. And considering the state of her nerves earlier today, who knew what her reaction to being accidentally married would be?

He knew very few lasses who would have dealt so well with all the mishaps they'd suffered in the past few days. Revealing this disaster could wait until tomorrow.

Braeden made his way through the crowd and up the stairs. He hesitated for a moment, then knocked on the door. Sarah responded, hiding behind the door, her head peeking out. "What do you want?"

He rested his hands on his hips. "I want to come into my

room."

She opened the door wider and stepped back. "Very well. But do whatever it is you need to do and then find where you will sleep." The lass drew herself up like the best matronly chaperone he'd ever encountered.

"Excuse me, lass?"

"Well, certainly you can't sleep in here." She swept her arm around to indicate the area.

"And why not?"

"Don't be ridiculous. We can't spend the night in the same room. It's not proper."

Little did the lass know how very proper it would be for him to spend the night here with her. Just the thought of climbing into the bed alongside her, pulling her warm soft body to his side, and making slow, sweet love to her drove his heartbeat up which, in turn, pumped all his blood to his lower parts.

"Ye just told the innkeeper we're husband and wife. Do ye not think the man will consider it strange if I go traipsing out to the stable to sleep with the animals?"

"I'm so sorry, Braeden. I didn't think about anything when I said we were married. I just wanted to get a room before they were all gone. I guess we could have taken the room for me and you could have stayed..."

"With the animals?" He shook his head. "Aye, 'twas a lot ye dinna think about when ye blurted out that we were married."

She waved her hand in dismissal. "It doesn't matter. We don't know anyone here, so we can tell a little bit of a lie." She chewed her lower lip. "Can't we?"

He sighed and ran his fingers through his hair. 'Twas still

a better idea to keep Sarah from knowing what she'd done. The lass had suffered one hardship after another, and what she needed now was food and a full night's rest. "Dinna fash yerself, lass. I will sleep on the floor, or the chair, but right now I will ask the innkeeper to send up a bath and some food. Ye need yer sleep."

She sat on the edge of the bed, her shoulders slumped. "There won't be a bath tonight, there are too many people here, and from the sound of the women I followed up the stairs, they are all wanting special treatment."

"Aye, I'm afraid yer right. I will go to the kitchen to get yer food and bring it up. That will give ye time while I'm gone to undress and climb into bed."

"Very well. I am too tired at this point to argue or wonder what everyone thinks." She gave him a slight smile. "Thank you. I appreciate your kindness."

"Aye, lass. Anything for *my wife*."

She picked up the slipper she'd just taken off and made a halfhearted attempt to toss it at his head.

"Before you go…" She twisted her fingers, embarrassed to ask the favor, but with the overflow of guests and the commotion they were causing the staff, she had no choice. "Can you help me out of my gown?"

Braeden's throat worked up and down, his features paling. "*Ach*, lass. Yer making things difficult for me. More so every minute."

She walked up to him and turned. "Please?"

What was she doing? She was in a room in the company

of a man not her husband, with the door closed, and he was about to undress her. Instead of fear, she felt an odd sort of excited anticipation. As if something was about to happen that she was unfamiliar with, but longed for. Parts of her body she was not usually aware of began to throb and swell. She felt damp between her legs, and her breathing hitched. What in heaven's name was happening to her?

She jumped when his warm fingers touched her back and slowly began to unfasten her gown. As each fastener released she caught her breath. Down his fingers moved, one hook at a time. When the last fastener had been released, she grasped the top of her gown to keep the bodice from dropping to her waist.

Even slower, his fingers worked to unlace her stays. His fingers fumbled, and she swore his hand shook. The sound of his panting only increased her awareness of whatever was happening between them. She could stand the silence no longer. "Braeden?"

"Aye, lass." He spread the panels of the stays, and she took a much needed deep breath. Before she could form any words, he kissed the side of her neck and pushed the gown off her shoulders. Any words she might have strung together flew out of her head like a flock of birds at the sound of a pistol shot.

"Ye are so beautiful, Sarah." He continued to kiss her neck, moving his lips down to her shoulders while his fingers pushed the sleeves of the gown toward her bent elbows. Taking both of her hands in his, he moved them to her sides so the silky fabric slid to her wrists and then off completely, the garment falling in a heap at her feet.

Her head fell back onto his chest as his hands cupped

her breasts, massaging the flesh, plucking at her nipples. She moaned and moved her head to the side as he nibbled at the soft skin behind her ear. Unhappy with the restriction of the stays, she tugged at the bottom of the garment, then shimmied until it, too, fell at her feet. Once it landed, Braeden scooped her up and strode to the bed, laying her gently on the mattress. He took her mouth in complete possession as he covered her body with his. His hands roamed over the dips and swells of her form, eventually settling his large palm on her bottom, rubbing circles over the sensitive area.

Sarah felt the bulge in his breeches pressing against the part of her that ached. She pushed back, rubbing against him to ease the throbbing. A groan escaped Braeden's mouth, and he brought his hand down to cup her most private part. She sucked in a breath when his fingers delved into the opening in her body that was moist and warm.

She should be embarrassed to have a man touch her where no one else ever had. But somehow it felt right, as if she knew instinctively his touch would lead to a place where she longed to be. That her body craved. Their remaining clothing became a restriction; she wanted to feel his skin against hers.

"Mrs. McKinnon, I have yer satchel here for ye that ye left downstairs." A woman's voice drifted through the door.

Sarah came back to herself with a jolt, reminding her of where she was and who she was with. And what they'd been doing. Oh God. What was the matter with her? "Get up." She pushed at Braeden's shoulders.

In a flash he was off the bed, shoving back the hair that had fallen on his forehead. His hands landed on his hips as he hung his head and took in deep breaths. Sarah swung her legs over the bed and stood, only to sit back down again. Her legs would not hold her.

"Mrs. McKinnon?"

"Yes. I will be right there." Was that her voice?

Braeden glanced down at himself and smirked. "I canna answer the door like this, lass."

"Oh." She felt the heat rise to her face as she once again attempted to stand. A little steadier this time, she managed to make it to the door on shaky legs and opened it, blocking her disheveled state from the woman. Reaching her arm out, she said, "Thank you," and took the bag from her hand.

"Did ye want me to send up a tray for ye, lass?"

"Nay." Braeden stepped to the door, apparently having recovered his dignity. "I was about to fetch my wife's dinner. 'Twill save ye a trip up and down the stairs."

Before Sarah had completely recovered herself, Braeden placed her satchel on the floor and left the room.

That man is dangerous. Very, very dangerous.

Feeling a bit more in control of himself, Braeden followed the woman down the stairs. The noise in the common room had ceased, but with all the gentry having retired to their rooms, the local townspeople were arriving for a night of visiting and drinking. What he needed more than anything was a swim in a very cold loch or a dousing in a trough.

Since only he, and not Sarah, kenned he had every right to make love to his accidental wife, it was best if he stayed away from her. The lass was obviously fatigued, so tomorrow after she'd refreshed herself with a good night's sleep would be soon enough to tell her about what she'd done.

The kitchen prepared a tray for Sarah that would help to restore the lass. He had them add a pot of tea, and then returned to their room. When he arrived, she had finished undressing and was in the bed, the covers pulled up and tucked under her chin. He grinned at her obvious message. And was happy about it.

Maybe.

"I have yer dinner. And a large pot of tea."

"Where is your dinner?"

"I want ye to eat in peace and get some much needed rest. I will take my dinner downstairs and expect ye to be fed and asleep when I return." He didn't add his main purpose was to throw cold water on his raging lust.

"Where will you sleep?"

Alongside ye so I can wrap my arms around ye in yer sleep and make love to ye first thing in the morning. "I will ask the innkeeper for extra blankets and curl up on the floor."

"Thank you. You are an honorable man, and I truly appreciate the respect you show me."

Ach, if ye kenned my thoughts ye would order me to sleep in the stables with the rest of the animals.

"Good night, lass." He closed the door and headed downstairs.

Once he had his dinner in front of him, his thoughts drifted to the problem the lass had presented them with by announcing in public they were married. Scotland's loose marriage law is what made midnight trips to Gretna Green so popular. He had no doubt, since she had spent a few Seasons in London, that Sarah was aware of that.

He pushed away his empty plate and considered how this affected him. He liked Sarah a great deal and respected the woman she was. He kenned with the strength of his convictions that she would make a more than pleasing wife. The intensity of their hunger for each other promised long nights of passion.

But what of his work? The letter that could very well already be waiting for him would be the culmination of all he'd worked toward. Was he prepared to give that up?

No.

Then there was Sarah herself and her edict that she had no desire, nor intention, to ever marry. She wanted to be the doting aunt to her sisters' and brother's bairns. Unnatural for a woman of Sarah's passion and caring. There had to be a story behind that intent.

Depending on how reliable the inn's horses for hire were, they only had one more night to spend together before they arrived at the MacBride home. He smiled at how well Sarah would take the news that they were married because of her slipup. Knowing her as well as he did at this point, he expected quite a battle. The lass had a great deal of fire in her. Fire he wanted to see directed at him in their bed.

Ach, what a situation I am in. A slow smile spread across his face.

Chapter Nine

The length and difficulties of the journey were taking their toll on Sarah. She was barely able to drag herself from bed when Braeden stood over her fully dressed and wide awake. "Come now, lass, the stable is readying our horses."

She covered her mouth to stifle a yawn. "Didn't we just fall asleep?"

"Nay," he grinned. "I came upstairs about ten last evening, and ye were slumbering away."

"What time is it now?" The yawn she'd tried to smother broke free.

"Half past six." He pushed his timepiece into his pocket. "I will see about the carriage while ye ready yerself." He got as far as the door and turned back. "Do ye need help in dressing?"

Yesterday's scene of them sprawled on the bed, Braeden's fingers doing delicious things to her body flashed in her mind.

Fighting the heat rising from her lower parts, she said, "No. I have a gown in my satchel that fastens in the front." No need to add she would also leave off her stays today, which only tied in the back. Although a proper lady never went beyond her bedroom door without her stays, it was better than what could occur if Braeden "helped."

Once the door was firmly shut, she fumbled in her satchel for her clothing. Of course, she'd lied to him. She would have to put a gown on backward and cover herself with her pelisse so she didn't look ridiculous. At least the air in Scotland, especially in the morning, was cool enough that she would need her warm pelisse, anyway.

Braeden greeted her as she made it to the bottom of the stairs. He looked the opposite of how she felt. Bright eyes, no evidence of sleep loss. And he'd spent the night on the floor! She couldn't help but wonder what her response would have been if he had crawled in beside her. Somehow she didn't think that was something she would have missed.

"I had a hasty breakfast set up for us in the private dining room."

Sarah took his arm and they proceeded into the room. A fire burned brightly in the stone fireplace in front of a table set for two. Once they sat, Sarah poured tea into her cup and Braeden's. "Ah, nothing tastes better to me first thing in the morning than tea."

"Yer verra English, lass."

She set her cup down. "Don't the Scots drink tea?"

"Indeed, we do. But I've never seen that look on any Scotsman's face while drinking tea. Now, if it were Scotch whiskey…"

A few more people, most likely from the large group of

travelers she'd seen yesterday, began to trickle into the room. Again, the older ladies were demanding special treatment, and had the serving girls scurrying to and fro, which had Sarah shaking her head.

Braeden regarded her over his cup of tea. "'Tis a bit warm in here. Perhaps ye should remove yer pelisse while ye eat."

"No. I'm fine. In fact, I feel a bit chilly." The sweat running down her face belied her words, but if she ate quickly, they would soon be in the carriage and on their way.

They did, indeed, make quick work of the porridge, sausage, and eggs. Just as they finished, the stableboy sent word through the serving girl that their carriage was ready.

Thank goodness. Sarah was about to expire from the heat of the fireplace and the warmth of her pelisse. Braeden pulled out her chair, and they headed to the front door. The cool air on her face felt wonderful, and she took deep gulps of it as Braeden helped her into the carriage. He had decided to ride Niels, so since there were no witnesses to her ruse, Sarah unfastened the pelisse and waved the flaps to cool herself.

At the sound of voices, she peeked through the carriage window to see Braeden shaking hands with another man. He was not quite as tall as Braeden and definitely rounder. It was a good thing he met the man on his way out instead of yesterday, so he didn't have to learn about her subterfuge in order to gain a room.

"Are ye ready, lass?"

At her nod, Braeden directed the driver to start off. Sarah leaned her head back, and feeling more comfortable with the pelisse opened and a full stomach, she closed her eyes and drifted off to sleep.

She jerked awake at the sound of the carriage door opening. Confused, she didn't quite remember where she was. She was cold, all the way to her bones. Then her memory returned. How she'd put her gown on backward to avoid Braeden's help and when she'd settled into the carriage she had opened the pelisse to cool off. It had worked, but now she was freezing.

Sarah pulled the pelisse closed and ran her palms up and down her arms. "Are we stopping?"

"Nay. A storm is starting up. I'll be joining ye for the rest of the trip." He settled in across from her. "Yer lips are blue and yer shaking. Ye seem rather cold. I hope yer not getting sick."

She shook her head. "I'm not sick. Just a little c-c-c-old." She moved the curtain aside to see the drizzle turn to steady rain pounding the ground, small pools of water quickly gathering on leaves. "Will the weather interfere with our drive today?"

"I hope not, lass. But if the roads become too muddy, the horses may have a hard time keeping their feet." He stretched out his long legs. "Only time will tell."

"If that m-m-m-message never reached her, my s-s-s-sister will be beside herself with w-w-w-worry."

Braeden grinned. "'Tis clear ye are more than a *little* cold." He reached out and pulled her to his side. "Here. Lean in to me, and we'll share the warmth." He opened his coat and wrapped it around her. The heat from his body seeped through her pelisse and gown, right to her skin, warming her immediately. But still she shook.

"I c-c-c-could use a cup of tea."

"Aye. I would love to have a whiskey myself, but we'll be lucky if we make it to another inn before nightfall. The driver has to go verra slow and careful along this path. Especially with the ground being so wet."

Sarah tilted her head to the side so she could look at him. "Is life always so difficult in Scotland?"

He threw his head back and laughed, then looked down at her. "Why do ye say that? 'Tis no harder here than anywhere else, I imagine. And probably a lot better."

She snuggled close to him again. "It just seems since I started this journey to see Sybil, so many things have gone wrong. I swear once I step foot in Bedlay Castle I will not leave for weeks." *Or until my publisher sends me word of my book release.*

"Are ye so sure you dinna want a life of yer own?" His voice softened. "Yer own husband, home, and bairns?"

The tingle that ran up her spine at his words disturbed her. He looked so earnest, and in some sense, even troubled. The path for her life had been set when she finished her book. She had known then that was what she wanted. When her publisher was so flattering in his enthusiasm for her writing, she'd known she'd made the right choice. Independence and freedom to write her stories.

No husband in Polite Society would allow his wife such liberty. She would do as she pleased, without the help of a man.

Well, except her publisher was a man.

But the time spent with Braeden had given her a glimpse of what she would miss. Not that she wanted to marry the Scot. The plans he had would never fit in with the life she had chosen. At least not for a number of years. Then again, the memory of his hands and fingers, and the expectation of what his lovemaking would feel like, warmed her almost as much as his nearness. It amazed her that they'd only known each other a few days. The smell of his body, the scent of sandalwood and horses, was already familiar and comforting.

His strong muscles as she leaned into him gave her a sense of security, of protection from all that was evil. She needed to be very careful around this man. He had her thinking about things best left alone.

"Sarah, there is something we need to discuss." Braeden sat up straight, his demeanor reminding her of the times her papa was about to dole out a punishment for some misdeed. Curious at his change in manner, she looked at him, but before he could speak, her thoughts were scattered as the carriage slid to the side and continued on until it landed abruptly against a large tree. Braeden's tight grip on her body kept her from flying about and landing on the floor.

"What was that?" She sat up and adjusted her bonnet.

"I would guess the carriage is not too steady on these roads. I will check with the driver." Braeden opened the door, and sheets of rain whipped in. He pulled up the collar of his coat, and with his head down, walked toward the front of the carriage.

The driver was just climbing down as he reached the horses. "Sir, I dinna think we can go much farther today. The horses are slippin' and slidin'."

"Aye. 'Tis pretty bad. Do ye know of any inns nearby?" Braeden shielded his eyes with his hand to keep the water out.

"Nay. I've been up and down this road many times. I only ken of a few cottages scattered here and there. We might find one who will take ye in for the night."

"Let's see how many miles we can put in today. But if it gets dangerous, we'll stop. Drive carefully, and go slow until ye see a cottage." Braeden splashed through mud, slipping until he grasped the door handle. He climbed into the carriage and wiped his face and spectacles with his handkerchief.

"What will we do now?" Sarah asked.

"The driver says there are numerous cottages around here. He is going to stop as soon as it appears too dangerous to continue on. Then we'll see if we can get the occupants to allow us to stay with them for the night."

"You're soaking wet!" She stared at the puddle of water at his feet.

"Aye. 'Tis a terrible storm out there."

They remained silent as the carriage crawled along. Time passed as Sarah shivered, the dampness from Braeden invading the carriage. She stayed huddled in the corner, wrapping her pelisse around herself in an attempt to keep warm. It wasn't working.

Eventually, the carriage came to a slow stop—more like a slide. She stared at the carriage door until the driver opened it. "I see a cottage down the path here, sir. I will knock on the door to see if they've room for ye."

"Nay." Braeden moved to step out. "'Tis only right for me to be doing the asking."

The walk was made soggier, if possible, by leaves from the trees overhead dumping their weight of water as he headed to the cottage. A tidy home, someone had laid a stone walkway from the edge of the woods to the front door. Large stone containers sat on either side of the door, holding flowers that drooped with the weight of the rain.

Braeden briskly knocked on the heavy wooden door. A slight overhang from the roof protected him from further dousing. The door opened and a large man, barrel-chested, with a full mustache and beard, smiled at him. "*Ach*, what are ye doing out in this weather, mon?"

"Good evening, sir. I am Professor Braeden McKinnon of Edinburgh University. I hate to disturb yer peace, but my wife and I are traveling to Bedlay Castle and our carriage can go no farther. I wonder if ye would be able to take us in for the night. We'll gladly sleep in yer stable if that is all right with ye."

The man peered at him. "McKinnon, ye say?"

"Aye."

"Margaret," he shouted over his shoulder. "One of the McKinnon lads is at the door. Wants to stay the night with his wife."

"Well, let them in, darlin'. Don't leave the poor things out there in the rain." A pleasant woman, almost as large as her husband, hurried up to the door, wiping her hands on an apron. "'Tis a pleasure to meet ye, Mr. McKinnon. Mr. Hanson and I would be happy to take care of ye for the night.

"My wife is still in the carriage. I wanted to be sure we would be welcome before I brought her out in the rain."

"Aye. Of course. Bring the lass in." The woman peeked around Braeden to eye the carriage at the end of their pathway.

"Thank you. And may our driver and footmen stay in yer stable?"

Mr. Hanson nodded. "There's a loft they can sleep in. Mrs. Hanson will send our boy out with supper for them."

"Thank you verra much." Braeden picked his way carefully along the stone path, slick with rain and wet leaves.

He opened the carriage door. "Let's go, darlin'. We will be warm and dry in no time."

Sarah peered out at the dark path leading to the brightly lit cottage. "Is it safe, just staying anywhere? We don't know these people."

"Aye. The man and his wife, Mr. and Mrs. Hanson, are agreeable people. He recognized my name, so I'm sure 'twill be fine. And at this point we have no choice."

She put one foot out the door and stopped. "Did you tell them we were married?"

"Aye. No reason not to."

She regarded him with furrowed brows. "I don't understand."

"Lass, I guarantee 'twill not be a problem. 'Tis a small cottage, there would not be two extra rooms." He tugged on her arm. "I'm getting verra wet out here, love."

"Oh, sorry." She climbed out and took his arm.

"Be careful, 'tis verra slippery."

After instructing the driver and footman on where they could stable the animals and bed down themselves, he led Sarah to the cottage door. Mr. Hanson stood at the portal holding a lantern to light the path as best he could without joining them in the rain.

"Good evening, Mrs. McKinnon. 'Tis a sorry night out there." Mr. Hanson moved back to let them enter.

The cottage appeared warm and friendly with a few

candles lighting the front area. The room had scarce furniture, worn, but clean. Mrs. Hanson had made it a pleasant and welcoming space. A bright rag rug in front of the fireplace caught sparks from the fire, and several embroidered pillows had been scattered about the room.

"Here, lass, let me help ye out of your pelisse. Ye can sit next to the fire and I'll bring ye a nice cup of tea." Mrs. Hanson approached Sarah and took over like a mother hen. She tugged the pelisse off Sarah and Braeden grinned. The lass's gown was on backward. Very inventive for avoiding his touch.

"Here, Mr. McKinnon. Mr. Hanson has some warm clothes ye can wear until yours dry out. Ye can change in the room on the left side. 'Tis our son Michael's room. Ye and yer wife can have that room." Mrs. Hanson handed him soft woolen pants and a warm woolen shirt. Then she turned to regard Sarah. "I'm afraid anything of mine would fit ye more like a blanket."

"That is all right," Sarah said. "I'm not nearly as wet as Mr. McKinnon. Just the bottom of my gown, and that will dry if I can sit by the fire."

"Aye, of course," the woman fussed. "Just sit right there, and I'll bring ye some tea. We'll be having our supper in a little bit, and that will help to warm ye up, too." She settled her hands on her generous belly and regarded Sarah. "So yer English, eh lass?"

"Yes."

Mrs. Hanson turned to Braeden. "So how did a fine Scottish lad such as yerself end up with an English lass?"

"'Tis a long story, Mrs. Hanson." Not wishing to dwell on their unexpected marriage, he added, "And 'tis grateful we are for yer hospitality." He left the room and immediately felt colder. The fire only warmed the main room, and he could see his breath in the air. The bedroom he had been directed to was clean and had all the appearance of a young boy's room. Space was precious in these small cottages, and it was not common for a lad to have a bedroom of his own.

Shaking from the cold, he stripped off his wet garments and drew on the ones Mrs. Hanson had given him. He used his damp shirt to dry his hair as best he could, then joined the others in the main room.

Sarah looked right at home, drinking tea in front of the fire and chatting with Mrs. Hanson. Mr. Hanson poured a small amount of whiskey into a glass and waved for Braeden to join him.

"'Tis fine whiskey I have here. Would ye care for a touch to warm yerself?" Mr. Hanson held up a stone container.

"Aye. I could use a bit of the warmth," Braeden said.

A lad of about fifteen joined them, shaking his wet coat until his mum chastised him. His da introduced him as their son Michael, who then proceeded to pick up a book and sit in the corner reading while the adults conversed.

As Mr. Hanson talked on and on, Braeden took the time to reflect on where he was at this point. Sometime tomorrow he and Sarah would arrive at Bedlay Castle. He would be fighting demons right now if he had to leave the lass there and go on his way. He'd grown fond of her and would miss her had things been different. But Sarah was his wife, and after a short visit with her sister, she would have to leave with him.

Truth be told, he was not looking forward to the conversation that would reveal what she'd done. He'd had time to accept this accidental marriage, and found himself pleased. His work would not suffer—he'd not allow that—but in addition to his work, he'd have Sarah. Thinking of the coming night in the cozy bed in the small bedroom had his cock hardening.

On the other hand, he had no idea how the lass would react to his announcement. They shared a strong attraction to which she was not immune. She seemed to like and respect him, and had already depended on him to protect her. But marriage?

Mrs. Hanson excused herself to finish supper. Braeden held out his hand to Sarah. "Are ye warm enough now? Would ye care to join us?"

"I do feel so much better." She rose and paced the few steps to where he and Mr. Hanson sat and settled on a small stool.

"Where are ye and the lass headed?" Mr. Hanson glanced longingly at his empty glass. He had already told Braeden his wife only allowed him one glass each evening. He'd winked when he'd passed that information along and chided Braeden to expect the same from his wife. "They all try to change yer bad habits, ye ken?"

"Sarah's sister is married to The MacBride, and we're headed to Bedlay Castle."

"*Ach*, Bedlay? Ye don't have much farther to travel, then."

"I will be glad to finish this journey. It has been quite tedious." Sarah glanced at Braeden for his confirmation.

Tedious, indeed, and also surprising. He had to bite the inside of his cheek to keep from laughing.

Chapter Ten

Despite her nap on the road, Sarah's head drooped as her hosts and Braeden talked quietly after supper. They were all seated in front of the fireplace, and she found it hard to stay awake. The soothing murmur of their voices washed over her like a lullaby.

"Lass. I think we need to retire for the night," Braden said, offering her a soft smile. "We want to be on the road early in the morning."

Mrs. Hanson sprang up. "'Tis sorry I am to keep ye up so late. I do tend to wander on when we have company, since 'tis so rare for anyone to happen by. Ye must be verra tired from yer journey. From what ye told us, 'tis been a trying one."

"Yes. It has been difficult, but it will be all worth it when I see my sister again." Sarah paused. "And her babe, who I am sure has been born by now."

"Aye. Nothing like a new bairn to bring more love and

hope to yer heart. I remember well when my Michael was born, he was such a—"

"Margaret, love, the young ones want to get some sleep." Mr. Hanson grinned at his wife whose rosy cheeks grew even rosier.

Sarah and Braeden wished the Hansons good night and entered the tiny bedroom they'd been given. Stopping abruptly, Sarah peered at the cold fireplace. "Goodness, it's cold in here. I can see my breath."

"Aye." Braeden leaned against the bedpost, his arms crossed over his chest. "Generally only in the dead of winter do these small cottages have a fire anywhere except the main room. 'Tis too costly to burn all that peat."

He pushed himself away from the bed and moved to stand in front of her, resting his hands on her shoulders. "Now, lass, I dinna want ye to get upset, but I will not be sleeping on the floor tonight."

Her mouth dropped open. "Why not?"

"Ye just said it yerself. 'Tis mighty cold in here. If I sleep on the floor—and survive till morn—I'll be too stiff to even move."

She glanced at the bed that looked very, very small. It would be impossible for them to both rest there without their bodies touching. She chewed her lip, remembering how difficult it had been to resist Braeden when he'd been helping her undress—while they both were standing up. "I have an idea."

He nodded for her to continue.

"We will sleep with all our clothes on, including our coats." She smiled brightly as if she'd just discovered the secret of life.

"'Tis fine with me. I will however, bring to your attention that scientifically, if a body were cylindrically shaped, and one ignored the losses on either end, the heat loss is in proportion to the circumference of each circle, divided by the circle area. Therefore the heat loss coefficient for each one is two/radius.

"Based on that assumption, if each cylindrical item—or person in our case—huddles alongside the other, the heat loss coefficient for the line is one/radius."

Sarah stared at him openmouthed. "I have no idea what you just said. What does that mean?"

"Body heat works very well and is better shared without too many layers of clothing. In fact, in the very cold climates, people oftentimes sleep side by side with no clothing at all."

She shook her head. "No. Never."

He flashed her a look she couldn't interpret. "Dinna fash yerself, lass. 'Twas only a suggestion." He waved in the direction of the bed. "Which side do ye want?"

Sarah moved to the right side of the bed and sat. "This side is fine."

Braeden toed off his boots. "Do ye want me to unfasten yer stays? I see ye put yer gown on backward. Verra clever."

"I thought I had my gown with me that fastened in the front, but I was mistaken." His grin told her he knew she was lying. "And no, I don't need your help since I didn't wear my stays today."

His smirk caused a wave of heat to race to her cheeks. She needed to climb into the bed, turn her back on him, and go to sleep. Although, for all the fatigue she'd felt a short time ago, now her heart was pumping, and she felt anything but tired. The tension in the air snapped like a fierce lightning storm.

She sat on the end of the bed and removed her shoes. Without turning to face Braeden, she lifted the covers and lay down, clinging to the edge, as far away from the middle as possible without tumbling to the floor.

The mattress shifted as Braeden settled in alongside her. Her hands were freezing; she should have left her gloves on. She thought about getting up and retrieving them from the dresser but didn't want to take a chance on attracting Braeden's attention. She tucked her hands between her thighs and began singing a song in her head, hoping to distract herself from where she was and who was with her, and possibly lull herself to sleep.

"Are ye humming?" Braeden's deep voice caused her to jerk.

"No."

"Aye, ye are."

"No, I'm not. I'm singing a song in my head."

"Then the tune is falling out yer ears, because I can hear it."

"I'm sorry if I'm disturbing you. I'm trying to lull myself to sleep."

She shut off the serenade. Next she practiced blowing air out to see her breath. It was very cold in the room. She puckered her lips to blow air, then opened her mouth wider to blow, amazed at the cloud coming from her lips.

"Are ye blowing out yer candle over there now, lass?"

"No." She rose up on her elbow and faced him. "Why don't you go to sleep and leave me alone?"

"I would be happy to, but yer making enough noise over there to keep the entire household awake."

She punched her pillow several times, wishing it was his face. "Oh, I doubt that very much. You do have a tendency to exaggerate, you know."

"I ken no such thing. Ye are singing and humming and blowing out air. I expect to feel yer feet tapping a dance soon."

Sarah expelled a huge sigh. "You can always sleep in the stables with the driver and footman."

"Nay, 'tis cold enough in here for me."

She felt him shift his body. "If you would lie still I might be able to go to sleep."

"*Ach*, lass, 'tis the first time I moved." He shifted once more, and she knew he was on his side, staring at her back.

She squirmed, uncomfortable with his scrutiny. Counting might help. She started with the rooms in Manchester Manor, starting at the top floor. The nursery, the nurse's bedchamber, the schoolroom, the governess's room. Next floor, her mother's suite of rooms, Drake and Penelope's—

"What are ye mumbling about?"

Sarah flipped over and drew in a sharp breath when she came practically nose-to-nose with Braeden. "What are you doing here?"

Raised eyebrows were his only response.

"I mean, you're so close. Can't you move back a bit?"

"Not unless I want to crash to the floor. Which I think will awaken Mr. and Mrs. Hanson, who are probably not sleeping anyway since ye keep making a racket over there."

She raised her chin, pushing her face closer to his. "I am not making a racket, and you are keeping me awake with all your chatter."

"Chatter?"

"Yes. You keep questioning everything I do."

"Perhaps because yer doing one senseless thing after another."

"I am not."

"Aye, ye are."

Her breath hitched as they both stared at each other. Heavy breathing filled the air, the puffs of moisture between them almost like a foggy day in London. Why were they both so out of breath?

Braeden lifted his hand and touched her cheek. "Yer skin is so soft, lass." He tracked down her cheek to her lips with his finger. She eased her tongue out and touched the tip. He tasted salty and sweet at the same time. Remnants, no doubt, from dinner. He traced her lips with his fingertip.

"Ye seem a little bit warm, lass. Perhaps ye should take off yer pelisse."

"Yes, I think you're right. I do feel a lot warmer than when we first came into the room." She sat up and unfastened the pelisse. Braeden helped her slip it off.

"I think I'll take my coat off as well." He quickly unbuttoned the garment and shrugged out of it.

Sarah lay back down. "That is much better. I don't feel quite so warm now."

Braeden was so hot at this point he could strip himself naked and still feel the need to dunk into a cool stream. Lying next to Sarah created a new definition for torture. He was trying so hard to ignore her, but her constant humming, moving, and talking made that impossible. Now all he wanted to do was take her into his arms and kiss every inch of her lush body. Pleasure her until she moaned his name and begged him to take her.

She continued to shift around and sigh.

"What is it now, lass?"

"I'm still too warm."

"Aye, you should probably remove yer gown and petticoat. Sleeping would probably be more pleasant if ye only wore yer chemise."

"How do you know what a lady wears under her gown?"

He grinned at her surprised expression. Surely the lass didn't think he was unschooled in the ways of intimacy? "I've had a wee bit of practice. Now sit up so I can help ye."

"I don't need help, thank you." Sitting up, she unfastened the backward gown, wiggling around until she was able to draw it over her head. Glaring at his interest in her performance, she turned her back to him as she worked the petticoat off, leaving only her chemise between her skin and his warm body.

"That is the very last article of clothing I will remove," she declared as she dropped the garment on the ground.

'Twas it him or herself she was trying to convince?

He stood and pulled his shirt over his head. Sarah's eyes never left his chest. Until his fingers rested on his fall front, and he slowly unbuttoned it, his eyes never leaving her, watching for her reaction. He almost groaned when she licked her lips. "Don't do that, lass."

"What?" She looked up abruptly, her lovely face guilt-ridden.

"Dinna look at me like that."

She stuck her cute wee nose in the air. "I was not looking

at you in any particular way."

Wearing just his drawers, he climbed into bed and stretched out on his back, his hands behind his head. Better to keep them away from Sarah. Within seconds, Sarah sighed. "I'm getting chilly now." She turned on her pillow to regard him. "Maybe I should put my gown back on."

"Nay." He reached over and pulled her body close to his. Precisely what he'd wanted to do since he'd first entered the bed. It felt right, like she belonged there, had always belonged there in his arms. He looked down at her. "Ye can share my body heat."

"You're not going to explain it all again, are you?"

"Nay." Was that frog-like croak his voice?

She wiggled closer. "Yes, you are warm." Using her fingernail, she scraped down his chest. "You have hair on your chest."

He inhaled as she tugged. "Does that hurt?"

"What hurts, love, is being here in bed with you and not able to do this." Giving in to his craving, he lowered his head and took her lips in a gentle, soft-biting kiss. He teased her lips until they opened, then slid his tongue into the warm, sweet place, loving the taste of her. Sarah joined in his duel of tongues, taking as much as she gave.

"The rest of yer clothes are getting in the way, lass," he murmured into her ear as he ran his tongue over the delicate shell.

She shook her head, but didn't stop him when he loosened the drawstring at the neckline of her chemise. Then she cooperated quite fully when he drew the garment up and over her head, tossing it on the floor. Gathering her into his arms, he held her snugly, her naked breasts flush against his skin.

Her skin was on fire and her heart hammered against his chest, beating in rhythm with his own. Spurred on by her response to his touch, he kissed her with his eyes before taking her mouth in complete possession, cupping her head to move it so he could delve deeper. She moaned softly and fisted his hair, tugging him even closer.

Releasing her lips he kissed her temple, then whispered into her hair. "Lass, ye do ken where this is going, aye?"

She pulled back and regarded him with half-lidded eyes. He was shocked at the impact of her look on his heart. No other woman he'd ever bedded had brought out the feelings he was experiencing with Sarah. 'Twas damn lucky for him she was his wife. If they made a bairn tonight 'twould be difficult with the expedition coming up, but they would make it work somehow.

"Yes, I have an idea what will happen next and I must admit, I'm frightened." The deep richness of her voice was a siren's call, but he needed to address her fears.

"Why, darlin'? Ye ken I would never hurt ye. At least naught more than nature intended." Concerned she might talk herself out of it, he ran his palm down her smooth skin to cup her breast. She sighed and closed her eyes. He lowered his head and suckled, pleasuring the engorged tip with his tongue.

She made little mewing sounds as he teased her nipples, going from one breast to the other.

"Braeden," she gasped.

"Aye, love. Just lie back and let me pleasure ye." He shifted so he covered most of her body.

She splayed her hands over his shoulders, molding the muscles before moving her fingers up to tangle in his hair.

Her touch overwhelmed his senses, bringing every drop of blood in his body to the one place he wanted to join with hers. His hands searched for her pleasure points, and he grinned as her soft sighs and frantic movements acted as a treasure map of her body.

Needing to rid himself of his drawers, he gave Sarah a quick peck on the end of her nose. "Dinna go anywhere, love." He hopped up and was free of the garment in seconds. Sarah's eyes grew wide at the evidence of his desire for her.

"Goodness," she breathed. But being Sarah, she reached out and touched him, encircling his manhood with her hand. "It feels strange. Soft, yet hard."

"Aye, love. Ye touching me this way feels strange." He placed his hand over hers as she began to draw away. "Nay. Dinna stop."

She studied her hand as she pleasured him, smiling when he let out a groan. "Does that feel good?"

"Aye. But if ye continue on, this could be all over before it begins."

"I thought you told me not to stop."

"Ye have me coming and going, lass. I dinna want ye to stop, but if ye dinna, ye won't have yer own pleasure." With that he eased her onto her back and once more took a plump breast into his mouth. His fingers worked their way down her smooth, silky skin until he reached the moistness of her center where he used his fingers to encircle, rotate, and enter her warmth to prepare her for their joining.

After several minutes, her restless movements told him she was nearing her release. He wanted more than anything to use his mouth and tongue where his fingers were so verra busy, but didn't want to scandalize the lass. Plenty of time for that once she accepted their marriage. Thoughts of all the wonderfully wicked things he could do to bring her pleasure heightened his desire to a point where he needed to take her before he disgraced himself.

As if she'd heard his silent plea, she stiffened and tightened her leg muscles, pushing hard against his hand. He covered her mouth with his to swallow her loud moan. No point in announcing to their hosts what they were doing in this room.

Relaxing her muscles, he used the opportunity to spread her knees apart and enter her in one swift thrust. Her eyes jerked wide, and he rubbed the bare skin of her shoulders.

"'Tis sorry I am, lass. That couldn't be helped."

She smoothed the hair off his forehead, taking in several deep breaths. Soon her muscles relaxed and she said, "It was all right. It only hurt for a second. In fact, now it feels… rather nice."

Gazing down at her, he braced himself on his elbows. She had still not caught her breath, and beads of perspiration dotted her forehead. She gazed at him, and his heart jumped. This seemed so right, having her beneath him. He would never grow tired of her or the pleasure he found in her arms.

He began the slow dance of lovers, flexing his hips and closing his eyes as he savored the feel of her warmth surrounding him. This was not like the mindless couplings he'd engaged in over the years. This was real, this felt like Sarah had claimed him completely. Mind, body, and soul. Having wanted her with such desire, he couldn't restrain himself, and with one final thrust, he threw his head back and groaned as he poured his seed into her.

Careful not to crush her, he rolled to the side and pulled

her close. The sound of their panting filled the air as his heart beat in rhythm with hers. Sarah wrapped her arm around his middle, snuggling close to his chest.

Braeden reached down and pulled the quilt up over them. "'Twill get cold in here verra soon, lass."

She stared up at him and licked her dry lips. "That was wonderful."

"Aye, I agree." He looked down, her flushed face and shining eyes taunting him with things he hadn't wanted for years. "'Tis glad I am ye think so, and honored to introduce ye to the pleasures of lovemaking."

"Is that what we did? Lovemaking?"

What exactly is the lass asking me? And do I have an answer I'm willing to give?

Chapter Eleven

Braeden had been staring at a sleeping Sarah for over an hour. He really should awaken her, but she looked so peaceful in her sleep. Her childlike countenance belied the passion in the lass he'd uncovered the night before. He'd known there were many layers to Sarah, and he'd been fascinated to uncover a few.

Just as the scant sunlight hit her face, she winced, and her eyes fluttered open. She sucked in a deep breath, and he could tell when the memories from the night before flooded her.

"Good morning, darlin'." Braeden pushed the hair out of her eyes and tucked it behind her ear.

"What have we done?" she whispered, fighting back tears.

"*Ach*, lass. Dinna fash yerself. 'Tis nothing wrong with what we've done." Of course she had no way of knowing there was naught wrong. The time had definitely come to let her in on their little secret. But with her determination to not marry, he didn't want to bring it up now and possibly cause a ruckus in their hosts' home. Once they were on the road, he would explain it all to her.

He didn't expect her to take the news well.

Her distress was understandable, since ladies of her station did not have sex with men to whom they were not married. Unless they were widows, or had indulgent husbands who looked the other way after an heir and a spare had been assured.

He would be no such husband.

"What I suggest we do is get dressed and be on our way. We are only several hours away from yer sister."

She winced once more as she moved to get up.

"Are ye sore?"

The tears she'd been fighting fell, sliding down her cheeks as she nodded. "Just a bit." Then she covered her face with her hands and sobbed. Braeden hopped off the bed and pulled on his drawers and breeches. If he attempted to soothe the lass he would blurt out what she'd done back at the inn, but he wanted her out of this cottage when that bit of news was revealed.

She needed warm water to ease the discomfort caused by the activity last night. It might even be painful for her to travel. At least today would not be a full day of riding.

"I will ask Mrs. Hanson for some warm water for ye. It will help ease the discomfort."

She wiped her cheeks with the sheet and nodded. "Thank you."

It unnerved him how important Sarah had become to him in such a short time. Whether because he knew she was his, or simply his attraction to her, he could not imagine the rest of his life without her. A complete turnabout from his plans up until about a week ago.

An hour later they were back on the road for the final leg of their journey. Sarah rode inside the carriage and he was on Niels. After the terrible weather yesterday, the new day was bright and sunny, the emerald green of the Highlands showing off its glory. He inhaled the air deeply, remembering, as always, how much he loved this land.

For just a moment he had a wisp of sadness at the thought of leaving Scotland behind for the two years of the expedition. He immediately shook off that feeling, since the expedition was more important to him than anything else in his life. He glanced at the vision of Sarah in the carriage attempting to read those blasted papers again. Maybe work was not the most important thing in his life anymore.

Pushing that thought aside, he reminded himself his work as a classical archeologist was how he identified himself. If that required him to live in places other than Scotland, then so be it.

What about my wife?

Dragging Sarah all over the globe for his work did present a problem. Then he excused his worry because 'twas her who had married them by declaring them thus in front of witnesses.

'Twas a problem he had been wrestling with as they grew closer to Bedlay Castle. Coward that he was, since they were so close to her sister, it seemed better to wait the extra hour or so to have Sarah with her sister when he lowered the boom.

Still deep in thought, he was startled to see Bedlay rise in front of them. They'd reached the end of their journey.

Once again he glanced down at Sarah gazing out the carriage window. He waved at her and pointed. "We're here, lass," he mouthed.

She smiled brightly.

Aye, darlin'. We're here and soon all hell will break loose.

S arah was stunned at how much she would miss Braeden. In the short time she'd known him, he'd become someone she'd learned to depend upon. She would miss his lively banter, his caring, and the power of his touch. Although, given what they'd done the night before, she should be glad to see them part. She'd been praying all morning that no consequences would result from their improper behavior.

But miss him, she would. Perhaps while she was staying with her sister, they could visit back and forth. However, the letter he so desperately waited for could send him off to the expedition in Rome at any time. A disturbing thought.

For now she relegated all of that to the back of her mind. Soon she and her twin would be reunited and she practically hopped up and down on the carriage seat like a young girl.

Bedlay Castle came into view. It was much bigger than she'd thought. It still amazed her that Sybil lived in a castle. Like a fairytale—which Liam and Sybil's story had been. He'd chased her all the way from Scotland to their home at Manchester Manor in the English countryside to convince her to marry him.

The carriage rolled to a stop and within seconds, Braeden was off his horse and helping her out of the vehicle. Her heart beat so fast in eagerness she actually felt dizzy. Finally, after all the mishaps, they were here.

"Sarah!" Sybil's voice drew her attention to the front door of the castle. Her sister stood with a babe in her arms, which she handed to an older woman standing next to her holding another babe. Picking up her skirts, her sister raced toward the carriage.

Sarah was almost thrown off her feet when Sybil slammed into her and hugged her so tight she couldn't breathe. Sybil pushed back, her hands anchored on Sarah's shoulders. "Where in heaven's name have you been? I've been worried sick."

"It is such a long story. You won't believe what we've been through."

"We?" Sybil just noticed Braeden standing behind her.

"Oh, Sybil. I'm sorry. This is Professor Braeden McKinnon." She drew Braeden forward. "Braeden, this is my twin sister, Sybil."

"*Ach*, lass, no one would have to tell me yer twins. If I wasn't so sure I was sober, I would swear I was seeing double."

"So the lass has finally arrived?" Liam strode up to the group. "Yer sister has been beside herself for days. 'Tis glad I am to see ye safe and sound." He turned to his wife. "I told ye not to worry, that yer sister was fine."

"Oh, you had no way of knowing that," Sybil chided.

"Didn't you receive a message that we were delayed?" Sarah asked.

Sybil shook her head.

Sarah turned to Braeden. "I told you that innkeeper wouldn't send the message along."

"Why are ye all standing about in the chilled air when we can be inside by the fireplace?" The older woman approached the group, the two sleeping babes still in her arms.

"Of course, Mum, we should all go inside. The sun will be gone in a little bit." Sybil wrapped her arm around Sarah's waist and propelled her forward. Liam took one of the babies from the older woman and led the group into the castle.

They proceeded down the corridor to a very warm, pleasant room. A fire burned brightly on the far wall in a huge stone fireplace. A chessboard was set up not too far away, with comfortable chairs and small tables scattered around the room. Two young girls advanced toward them, shy smiles on their faces.

"Let's all sit down, and we can catch our breath. Mum, will you ring for tea for our company?" Sybil took the babe from the older woman's arms. She looked at the baby and then up at her sister and burst into tears.

"*Ach*, lass. Ye surely have turned into a watering pot." Liam sat next to her and juggled the baby in his arms so he could put his other arm around his wife's shoulders.

"You look so much like Sybil," the younger of the two girls said, her mouth agape as she stared at Sarah. Both girls and their mother had arranged themselves on a rose damask settee. Sybil and Liam sat side by side on another settee, each with a babe in their arms.

Sybil wiped her eyes on a handkerchief Liam handed her, then blew her nose. "All right. I feel better now. I think we should introduce everyone.

"Sarah, you know Liam. This is his mother, Lady MacBride, his sisters, Catriona and Alanna." The older woman and two girls stood and dipped a slight curtsy.

"And here we have…" Sybil opened the blanket covering the baby she held. "Our daughter, Andrina." Before Sarah could say anything, Sybil moved the blanket from the other baby's face and said, "And our son, Donald."

"Twins." Sarah burst out laughing. "How wonderful."

It had just occurred to her that all this time Braeden had remained silent. Of course, he was probably anxious to deposit her with her family and leave. She fought down the tears that threatened and looked over at him where he stood leaning against the door, his arms crossed.

"Liam, I would like to introduce you to Professor Braeden McKinnon." She walked to where he stood and took his hand, bringing him closer to the gathering.

Liam's head snapped up. "McKinnon, ye say?"

"Aye," Braeden answered.

"Braeden?" Liam's eyes narrowed. "Aren't ye the genius lad?"

Braeden grinned. "I'm afraid 'tis me."

Liam handed his son to Sybil and stood to shake Braeden's hand. He turned to Sybil. "The lad here is cousin to Laird Duncan McKinnon."

"Oh, how nice to meet you." Sybil smiled at him. "My close friend, Lady Margaret, married your cousin about a year ago, now."

"Yes, I ken. I was detained at university and couldn't make the wedding."

Liam slapped Braeden on the back. "So how is it ye arrived with Sarah?"

Sarah shook her head. "You would not believe all the trouble we've had." She began counting off on her fingers. "First our carriage crashed, killing the driver and footman accompanying me."

"Oh, no!" Sybil gasped. "Who?"

"Not one of ours. Drake hired them for the trip. It was very sad, though. I felt horrible." She paused for a moment. "Then Braeden happened by and accompanied me and my lady's maid, Alice, to a nearby inn."

"That was verra nice of ye, lad." Liam nodded his approval.

Sarah continued. "Braeden hired a new carriage and driver for us and we continued on. After only a day or so Alice became very ill with typhus."

"My goodness, how awful for her. Is she recovered yet?" Sybil said.

"No. The healer who attended her said she needed to stay in bed for a couple of weeks. So Braeden and I continued on. I told Alice we would send a carriage back for her when we arrived here."

Liam moved to a large wooden desk in the center of the room and leaned his hip against it, his arms crossed. "So just ye and the lad here traveled alone?" He gestured with his chin toward Braeden.

"Yes, but it turned out fine. Well, except when we were held up by highwaymen."

Sybil's eyes grew wide. "You certainly did have quite a troubled journey. Did anything else happen?"

"No, thank goodness. Aside from a cracked wheel that needed replacing and bad weather that forced us to stay with a lovely couple for the night, we finally made it here."

"*Ach*, lass. Ye left out one important event on our trip." Braeden sat alongside her and took her hand in his.

Sarah gave him a questioning look. "What?"

"We got married."

Chapter Twelve

The silence from the group in the room was deafening. Sarah stared at Braeden openmouthed while he only grinned.

"My lady, here is your tea." A tall, balding man entered the room, carrying a large tray with tea. Behind him followed an older woman with a younger girl, both of them carrying trays of sandwiches and cakes.

"Just put it over there, please," Lady MacBride said, waving in the direction of a long, narrow table against the wall.

Once the door closed on the servants, Sarah yanked her hand from Braeden's. "What are you talking about?"

He stood and paced, running his fingers through his hair. "Ye married us at the inn we stayed at that was crowded with the guests on their way to the wedding."

"I did no such thing." Her heart pounded as if it planned to jump from her throat and run around the room screaming and pulling its hair out. Married? Was he suffering from a brain fever?

Liam spoke from where he stood by the desk. "Lad, I think ye better explain yerself."

Braeden took a deep breath. "When we arrived at the inn, 'twas crowded with travelers on the way to a wedding. There was only one room left. Sarah announced to the innkeeper and anyone nearby that one room would be fine because we were husband and wife."

"You said that?" Sybil looked aghast.

"Well, something like it. The innkeeper assumed we were married, and I didn't correct him. If we didn't take the room we would have had nowhere to sleep. It was late, and the next inn was hours away."

Braeden went down on one knee and took her hand. "Lass, according to Scottish law, if ye declare yerself married in front of two witnesses, 'tis a valid marriage."

"That's ridiculous. It can't possibly be that easy to marry." She pulled her hand away. "And it doesn't matter, because I don't know the innkeeper, and he would have no reason to remember me or what I said."

"But the innkeeper kenned me. Do ye remember?" Braeden said. "Also the innkeeper referred to ye as my wife when I was speaking with a member of that wedding party who knows me and my family. And last night we stayed with Mr. and Mrs. Hanson in their cottage. We shared a bed, lass. 'Tis considered a consummated marriage."

"Catriona and Alanna, leave the room," Liam growled.

At the sound of their brother's voice the girls hurried to the door, giggling between them. "Mum, please take the bairns upstairs to their nurse. It appears we have something to settle here."

Sarah was in shock. Married? No. It could not be that easy to marry someone. Furthermore, she had her life planned, and it did not include a husband. And most of all, not Braeden McKinnon who had plans of his own that would most definitely clash with hers. Perspiration dotted her forehead, while her hands felt clammy. Perhaps she was getting sick, after all.

"Lass, I think ye should put yer head between yer knees. Ye look pale," Braeden said.

Liam moved to stand in front of Sarah and Braeden. "If ye declare yerself married and stayed together in a room, yer married, lass. That's the way of it."

"No." Sarah hopped up. "I don't want to be married. I am not married. I refuse to be married." She plopped right back down when dizziness threatened to overcome her.

As if he sensed her delicate state, Braeden wrapped his arm around her shoulders. "We are married, Sarah, 'tis done and nothing can undo it."

She rounded on him, her heart pounding. "It's your fault. You should have stopped me when I told the innkeeper we were married."

"Stop you? You kicked me when I asked ye to repeat yerself."

"What sort of a man are you that a little bit of a kick would keep you from saving us from this disaster?"

"Disaster!" he growled. "Is that what ye think?"

"Well this is certainly not something you or I wanted."

"Whether we wanted it or not, 'tis done!"

"By the saints!" Liam shouted. "Ye are both brawling like a couple of bairns." He turned to Sarah. "I hate to come down so hard on ye, since we are barely acquainted, but not only are ye married, I will be bringing Father O'Reilly to Bedlay as soon as possible to bless the marriage."

Sarah gaped at him. "What? Why would you do that?"

"Because I am yer laird and head of yer family here. Ye spent time alone on the road with McKinnon, and according to him, shared a bed. I have no interest to ken what happened in that bed, but 'tis enough for me to demand ye marry properly so there will be no doubt."

Sarah felt her cheeks warm at the memories Liam's words brought, which he apparently noted. His snort told her so. "Aye, lass. 'Tis time for a proper wedding."

"You can't order me to marry." She crossed her arms over her chest.

"Aye, I can, and I will. And ye ken in yer heart that were ye brother here, he'd be doing the same thing." He straightened, his hands on his hips, very much The MacBride. "I stand in his stead."

Directing his attention to Braeden, he said, "I will notify the Duke of Manchester of the situation, and as soon as I have the marriage contracts and Sarah's dowry in hand, I will notify you."

Sarah looked pleadingly at Sybil. "He can't make me do this."

Sybil wrung her hands. "I'm sorry, Sarah. So sorry. But surely you have heard about the loose Scottish marriage laws from the scandals of couples racing off to Gretna Green to be married. And I'm afraid Liam is right. You know, as well as I do, that if Drake were here he would be demanding a proper wedding."

Sarah glanced at Braeden who was still on one knee

beside her. Once again he took her hand and held firm when she tried to withdraw it. Looking at her, he addressed Liam. "Laird, may I have a few moments alone with my wife?"

"I am *not* your wife."

"Come, love. Give them some time together to get this sorted out." Liam took Sybil's hand and led her from the room. Sybil looked back at her twin as they slipped through the door, mouthing the words *I love you.*

As soon as it closed, Sarah glared at Braeden who looked as if he were trying to form the right words to say.

There are no right words.

"I ken this is a shock to ye, lass. I dinna tell ye when it happened because ye were so tired and anxious about arriving here." He tilted her chin up. "Is the idea of marriage to me so terrible for ye?"

"You don't understand. I was very clear about my intention to never marry. I don't want a husband. I have other plans for my life."

He rose and sat alongside her. "And what plans do ye have that marriage would interfere with?"

Should she tell him? Reveal the secret that even her twin didn't know? She had planned to share her news with Sybil once she settled in. But her publisher told her a four or six week trip to visit with her sister would give him enough time to get her book ready for print. He expected her back in London at that time so she could do newspaper interviews and be available to meet readers and sign her books at the bookstores in London and the surrounding areas.

On the other hand, if she were forced to take a husband—and it appeared that was exactly what Liam had in mind—there could be many other men who would be a worse choice. Therein lay the problem. If she didn't already care for Braeden, she could convince him to have a marriage in name only, and they could live separately so she could pursue her dream. But he was a warm, honorable man, and he deserved more. More than she was prepared to give right now.

Part of her was terrified at growing too fond of him, and another part of her didn't want him to walk away. What a conundrum she'd created with her flippant words back at the inn. And why was it she'd not remembered about Scottish marriage laws? Sybil was correct. There had certainly been enough gossip about *ton* couples running off to Gretna Green to marry against family wishes.

This time the marriage had been performed against the bride's wishes.

She drew herself up. "My plans are to have independence, apart from the demands of a husband. There are things I want out of life that would be stifled by marriage."

"Yer not making sense, Sarah, and I'm thinking right now ye should get some rest. We can deal with these little problems later. Yer exhausted from the trip, and I don't think ye are thinking clearly."

Little problems! How dare the man dismiss her so readily? Obviously, he would dismiss her hopes and dreams as easily, too. Well, far be it from her to share anything about her writing with the man.

"Very well. I will take my *little problems* to my bed-chamber to rest, as my lord and master has ordered." She swept past him and headed to the door.

"Sarah."

She kept going, enjoying the sound of the library door

closing smartly.

Sarah awoke to a day she'd thought would not happen for several years, if at all. Her wedding day. Although, according to Scottish law, that day had already come and gone without her knowledge. She still fumed at how blasé Braeden was about the entire thing. Marriage was a huge step, and she didn't want to be married. Not unless she could have the life she had planned.

She'd never gotten the chance to talk to Sybil privately yesterday, with all the flurry of unpacking, taking a tour of the castle, and settling in. Then all the family had gathered for dinner, along with clan members, followed by singing and dancing to celebrate their arrival, until Sarah thought she would drop.

Liam's mother and sisters were delightful, and they obviously adored Sybil. A far cry from how things had started off for her twin. A slight scratch at the door drew her from her musings.

Sybil stuck her head in. "I brought you a gown I think will look wonderful for your wedding." She held up a lovely pale yellow gown with deep yellow and green embroidery on the sleeves and hem. A green satin ribbon was tucked underneath the bodice.

"It's beautiful."

Sybil settled on the bed and regarded her twin. "How are you faring?"

"Not well. Not at all."

"You know, I don't understand your dislike for marriage.

I remember as young girls we would talk well into the night about the 'knight in shining armor' in our future, falling in love, and our wedding day. Do you recall we promised to have a double wedding?"

Sarah shrugged.

"Then a few years ago you started spouting all this nonsense about being the 'doting aunt' and not wanting to tie yourself to a man. What happened?"

"I have other plans. Things have happened since we were girls." She was enjoying the perplexed expression on Sybil's face.

"What 'things'? I know everything about you."

Sarah smiled. "Not everything, dear twin sister. You know how I've been keeping a journal?"

"Yes, you've kept one almost since you were able to hold a pencil."

Unable to sit still while sharing the one thing that belonged only to her, she stood and wandered around the room, dragging her fingers over the dresser. "I stopped writing in my journal a few years ago."

"Nonsense, you've been scribbling daily for years."

Sarah turned to face her twin. "Yes. I was writing stories."

"Stories?"

Sarah grinned. "Don't laugh, but I've been writing stories of romance."

If the expression on Sybil's face was any indication of how the rest of her family would deal with her secret pastime, there were a lot of surprised looks in her future.

Sybil placed her hand over her chest. "Romance stories?"

"But there is even more news."

Her twin gestured for her to continue.

"One of my stories is being published!" Sarah hadn't realized how proud she was of herself until she saw the look of surprise and admiration in her sister's eyes. Sybil covered her mouth with her hands and began to laugh. Then she jumped up and hugged Sarah.

"Do you mean to tell me I'm the twin sister of an author?"

"Yes!" They held on to each other, giggling while jumping up and down, much like they had done in their youth.

Arms wrapped around each other, they fell backward on the bed, wiping tears of laughter from their eyes. After a few minutes Sybil raised herself up on her elbows. "But you still haven't told me why you don't want to marry Braeden. It's obvious you care for each other. Just the short time I spent with the two of you, it was obvious…"

Sarah took a deep breath. "My publisher wants me in London when my book is released so I can speak with newspaper people, meet readers, and sign books. Michael Dunsten—that's my publisher—is very forward thinking and believes women have the ability to do just about anything they choose."

"You actually found a man who thinks that way?"

"Yes, isn't it wonderful? He is already pushing me to finish my second book. He has an office in London, and I've met with him a few times while his company was working on my book."

Sybil frowned. "Is there more than just your book between you and this man? Is that why you don't want to be married to Braeden?"

Sarah waved her hand. "Not at all. Heavens, you make me laugh even suggesting that. Mr. Dunsten is old enough to be my grandfather and indeed does have grandchildren."

She sat up and bent her knees, hugging them close to her chest. "Don't you see, Sarah? If I have a husband, I won't be able to return to London when I need to. He might even forbid me to write and publish."

"You have no reason to believe Braeden will make you stop writing."

"But you remember he mentioned he is waiting for word that he's been accepted for an archeological dig in Rome?" She stood again, her hands on her hips. "He will expect me to go with him, and I can't go to Rome."

Sybil rose and placed her hands on Sarah's shoulders. "You need to speak with Braeden about this. From the way you talk I'm assuming he doesn't know?"

Sarah shook her head. "You are the first person I've told."

"Then talk to him." She leaned forward and kissed her on the cheek. "You might find you have no problem at all. But now, it is time for you to dress for your second wedding."

Braeden checked his timepiece once more. Weddings made him very nervous, and this one was no exception. Except 'twas a mere formality since the lass had married them already. But, somehow, facing his family and friends and standing before the priest made it all seem more real. He was grateful for Liam's insistence on the service, however. Sarah was a reluctant enough bride, without having her forever arguing that they were not *really* married. He envisioned years of spirited disputes with the lass. And interesting ways to make up afterward.

His cousin, Duncan, slapped him on the back. "'Tis a day I never expected to see, lad. Ye always had yer nose stuck in a book, and busy pondering them ancient *Sluagh*. Didn't think the lasses interested ye."

"Oh, the lasses interested me all right. I was just holding out for the right one."

"And ye think Sarah is? I understand the lass tied the knot with words tossed about in public and before ye kenned it, ye were shackled."

"Aye. 'Twas pretty much that way. But 'tis not sorry I am. She's a fine lass and I think we will do well together."

"Good luck." Duncan moved away as he was summoned by an elder aunt.

I think we will do well together.

Right now that was more a wish than a certainty. She hadn't spoken to him since Liam had laid down his edict about them having a wedding ceremony. She'd immediately left the room with her sister in tow. The rest of the day had been spent with crowds of people surrounding them. Each time he'd tried to catch her eye, she had turned to speak to another. *On purpose?*

Since that was only last evening, he couldn't honestly say she was avoiding him, but at breakfast this morning, she and Sybil had their heads together, which his sister-in-law advised him were wedding plans.

Braeden had been more than a little annoyed when Liam informed him he would not be allowing Braeden to sleep with Sarah until the priest had come and gone. His only consolation was Liam's tale of how Sybil's brother, Drake, had not permitted Liam anywhere near Sybil until the ceremony, even though the lass was already increasing.

"'Tis time to gather." Liam stood at the front of the large hall that had once been three times its size before the laird had divided the space into a dining hall, smaller family dining room, a parlor, and a library.

A few members of both the MacBride and the McKinnon clans were present, mostly those from the MacBride clan since many of them worked at the castle. His mum and da made the short trip with his brother, Evan, and his sisters, Fiona and Morna. His other two brothers, Morgan and Fraser, had been unable to attend on such short notice.

Braeden moved to the front of the room with Evan at his side. Mumbled voices behind him told him that Sarah had entered the room. He turned and his breath caught. Even though she and Sybil were twins, Sarah was so much more beautiful to him. Her gown of pale yellow flowed from underneath her plump breasts to the tips of her deeper yellow slippers peeking out.

Her silky brown curls, interspersed with a white ribbon, were pulled back from her sweet face to tumble down her back. With Sybil next to her, the two of them joined him and Evan. He took her ice cold hands in his and gazed into her eyes. Eyes full of uncertainty.

"'Tis all right, lass." He said as he bent to brush the words next to her ear.

Her slight smile turned into tightened lips, which confirmed his belief that she was angry at being forced to stand here in front of friends and family and acknowledge their accidental marriage.

It only took a matter of minutes for them to complete the ceremony, which left Sarah appearing unsettled. Despite her reluctance, he bent and kissed her, happy she didn't pull away or turn her head.

Liam's cook, Mrs. MacDougal, provided a hearty breakfast that all the guests enjoyed. While Sarah wasn't exactly friendly toward him, she at least didn't stab him with her fork, although he did keep a keen eye on her knife.

"Are ye coming home tonight, lad?" His da stood with the other members of his family as they took their leave.

"I'm not sure. I think Sarah would like to spend some more time with her sister, but there are things I need to take care of at home. Did ye notice a letter for me from the Royal Society of Edinburgh?"

"Nay. Ye have a bit of mail at home, but I dinna remember anything with that name on it."

Braeden shook his father's and brother's hands and kissed his sisters. "I will be home as soon as I can wrestle my wife from her sister. They haven't seen each other in quite a while."

"A lovely lass, yer Sarah is. I think she will make ye a fine wife." With those departing words, his mother kissed him on his cheek and joined the rest of his family in their wagon.

As he watched his family ride away, speaking lively with one another, he again felt the sense of isolation that had been part of his life since he'd been a lad. He was so different from the rest of them. They were all hard-working, respectable, and honest. "People of the Land," his da often called them. He, on the other hand, was not happy unless he was delving into ancient tomes and losing himself in libraries and museums.

Mathematical equations and scientific explanations were far more interesting to him than crops and sheep illnesses. Thankfully, his parents had allowed each and every one of their six children to follow their hearts. But he was the only one who hadn't followed the rest of them. Nevertheless, he loved them completely and respected his parents and their life. It just wasn't his.

He headed back to the main hall in search of Sarah. She stood with Sybil and Liam, speaking with Lady MacBride. Liam's two sisters each held a bairn, with their mother providing oversight. He loved the story Liam had told him of how his mum had been against him marrying Sybil and had caused quite a bit of trouble for the two of them before she took Sybil under her wing. It was nice to hear there were some happy endings.

"Lass, I'd like to leave for home before it grows dark. The laird has offered the use of his carriage."

Sarah chewed her lip. "May I speak with you in the library?"

"Of course." She swept past him, and he followed her out of the hall and down the corridor to the library.

She opened the door and turned to him. "I asked Liam if it would be all right for us to talk in here."

He frowned as she twisted her fingers. So she'd been planning this, since he hadn't seen her speak to Liam. What did the lass have in mind now? She walked behind the settee, obviously not wanting them to be seated together. All right, if she would stand, so would he. "What did ye need to say to me that we had to have a private place to speak?"

"I want to stay here with Sybil." Once the words were out, she seemed to relax as if the words themselves were as unwelcome as her intent.

Not one to rush his answers, he thought for a moment, noticing she grew uneasy as he continued to study her. Before he gave a hasty answer, he asked, "Why?"

"Because I came all this way to visit with my sister, and spend time with her and the babe. Well, babes, actually. I didn't know she'd had twins. I know from my mother that twins are a lot of work, and even though she has a nanny—"

"Yer blathering, lass. Make yer point."

"My point is I hadn't planned on marrying, and even though we have—married—I don't see any reason why I should change my plans. I did come all this way to see my sister."

"Aye. That ye did." He walked around the settee, both amused and annoyed when she edged her way behind it, so they were still separated by the piece of furniture. "And how long do ye think ye need to stay here with yer sister?"

Sarah shrugged. "I don't know. A few weeks, perhaps."

"A few weeks! Ye expect me to leave and have ye stay here for a few weeks? Lass, ye have to reconcile yerself to the fact that whether ye intended it or not, we are married. I expect ye to pack yer belongings and go with me to Dundas Castle where I keep a room until I hear about the expedition I hope to secure."

She stuck out her chin. "And then what?"

The lass had him there. He had no idea what the answer to that question was. What would he do?

"That has yet to be decided. Right now I'd like to know why my wife is so reluctant to be married."

"And what exactly does that mean?"

Before she could react, he grabbed her arm and tumbled her into him until they both fell on the settee, her sprawled on top of his body. "Now this is the position I want us to be in." He raised his head up and took her lips in a searing kiss. She struggled a bit, but then sighed and relaxed.

Her softness against the hardness of his body woke up his neglected manhood. He shifted to get more comfortable, so they were side by side, the blood racing to his erection with lightning speed. His hands roamed over her body, making circles on her back, growing closer to her bottom. His fingers worked her gown, edging the hem up until he reached the soft skin above her stocking.

Moving her slightly, he continued his journey, his hand sliding upward, until he reached her warm, moist center. "*Ach*, lass. Yer ready for me," he whispered into her mouth.

Sarah moaned, her fingers delving into his hair. "We can't do this here. Someone could come in."

"Aye. I agree with ye." He rose, taking her with him. The hem of her gown fell to her feet and she stared at him with half-lidded eyes. "We'll retire to yer bedchamber and take up this discussion tomorrow."

When she looked as though she would argue the point, he swept her weightless into his arms and strode to the door.

He bent to open the latch, then entered the corridor, heading toward the stairs. Taking the steps to the next level two at a time, he stopped at the top of the stairs. "Which way to yer room?"

"Third door on the left," she murmured.

Deciding it was best to keep her occupied so she didn't overthink the situation, he reclaimed her lips, crushing her to his chest. A young maid was just exiting the room Sarah stated was hers. She scooted out of the way and continued on, leaving the door ajar, making it easy to enter the room and kick the door closed with his foot. He proceeded directly to the bed, tumbling Sarah onto the mattress and following her down.

"Let me help ye out of yer gown, darlin'."

"My maid—"

"Just left. I'll be yer maid." His stiff fingers unfastened her gown and untied her stays in record time. Soon she was left in her stockings and nothing else except the white ribbon in her hair. He propped himself up on one elbow as he ran his hands over her naked form, stopping to tweak her nipples, then moving down to her nest of dark curls.

His wife. The words resonated in his brain. No worries about not taking their time, or about making noises. 'Twas his wedding night, and he had many things planned for his bride. He hoped to have her wholly scandalized and thoughts of staying with her sister gone. He would make slow, sweet love to her until she cried his name and begged him to grant her release.

He would take her, over and over, until the sun crept beyond the horizon and he had made her so completely his that she would follow him anywhere.

Chapter Thirteen

Sarah lay on her side, her hands tucked under her cheek as she stared at her husband lying on a pillow next to her. He was sleeping peacefully, looking younger with his spectacles sitting on the table next to the bed.

Memories of last night, and the several times they'd made love in so many different ways, caused her heart to thump madly. Both with passion and fear. If she spent more nights like that with this man she might very well end up in a family way, which would bring a halt to all her plans and dreams. Leaving her right where she swore she would not be. However, since he was expecting to leave the country for two years once he received the acceptance she was certain he would obtain, she only had to hold him off for a short time.

Once he was on his way to Rome, she could wait here with her sister until she received word from her publisher. She'd be able to enjoy her niece and nephew and finish the next book. She sighed and rolled over to stare out the window at the beautiful summer day. Scotland was truly a lovely place, and in some ways she would be sorry to leave it behind.

The mattress shifted, and then warm lips settled on her nape, alerting her to Braeden's readiness to resume where they'd left off the night before. She closed her eyes and edged away. The best time to start detaching herself from him was now. "I am a bit sore. Perhaps I need to send for some warm water."

"Of course," he murmured. "I don't want to cause you any pain."

She left the bed and shrugged into her dressing gown before summoning a maid. They'd sent a carriage for Alice yesterday, but it would be a week or more before she could expect her to arrive.

Braeden threw off the covers and stood, running his fingers through his hair. Sarah's breath hitched at the sight. The sun streaming through the window highlighting his form left her mesmerized. He could pass for any statue in the museum of Greek gods. Except he was human, and all warm flesh and sinewy muscle. His unfashionably long wavy black hair covered his ears and fell in disarray over his forehead. She darted her eyes away, not wanting him to see her admiring him.

"I will head back to the room Liam relegated me to and dress." He pulled on his breeches and tugged his shirt over his head. He hesitated as if wanting to say something and then merely nodded and left the room.

Sarah let out a deep breath. So far, so good. Now to convince him he should return to Dundas and leave her with

Sybil. Her water arrived and she washed, using the warm cloth to ease the tenderness between her legs. Touching herself brought back memories that had heat rising to her face.

How Braeden had used his mouth and tongue in places on her body that had scandalized her. Although it had felt wonderful at the time. He'd told her there were many other ways he could pleasure her.

Best to forget those.

Liam, Sybil, Lady MacBride, Catriona, Alanna, and Braeden were sitting at the breakfast table when she arrived. Sybil grinned in her direction which once again brought heat to Sarah's face. They didn't have to be twins for her to know why Sybil was grinning.

Sarah filled her plate from the side table with a boiled egg and toast. It was easy to pass up the porridge and haggis, something she was sure she would never favor. The little bit of food and several cups of hot tea restored her and prepared her for the confrontation with Braeden.

Braeden wiped his mouth with his serviette and placed it next to his empty place. "Lass, we need to depart today."

Apparently, yesterday's conversation hadn't worked too well. She decided to try a different tactic. She took a deep breath, then gritted her teeth as she took a submissive demeanor. "I would like permission to stay with Sybil for a while. I had planned to spend time helping and enjoying her babes, and I still want to do that. At least for a little while."

She ignored her sister's snort at her little act as Braeden sat back and regarded her. A flash of annoyance ran through her at the grin he tried to suppress. Obviously, he found her submissive demeanor not only unbelievable, but humorous.

He shook his head, and his grin grew wider. "Permission, lass? Aye, I can understand that. 'Twould be unfair of me to insist that ye leave when we've only just arrived." He continued to study her while Sarah held her breath.

"I wish I could stay here with ye. Unfortunately, with all the preparations I need to make for the expedition, and research and correspondence I am far behind on, I am in need of Duncan's extensive library. 'Twould be time consuming to travel back and forth each day.

"If the laird agrees, ye can stay for a bit to visit with yer sister. Perhaps I can take some time to visit with ye."

Sarah breathed a sigh of relief, reminding herself this was precisely why she didn't want a husband. Why should she have to ask permission to visit her sister?

Now if she could stay here until Braeden's letter arrived, she would be safe. He would go off on his expedition, and she would stay at Bedlay until she received word from her publisher.

Braeden could not deny how annoyed he was at the relief in Sarah's expression when he agreed that she could stay with her sister. Last night, he'd been able to distract her from her intention, but tossing her over his shoulder now and hauling her upstairs in front of her family for a repeat was not the best idea.

This marriage was not starting off well. He understood the lass's sense of betrayal. But the right opportunity to tell Sarah what she'd done hadn't presented itself until they'd arrived two days ago. For whatever reason, she was reluctant to be married and was having some problem adjusting to the idea. So very different from how he'd viewed her since they'd met.

She'd been strong, and able to handle situations that most ladies of her station would have been wailing and swooning about. Her stamina was one of the many things about her he admired. But she had fallen completely apart at the news of their marriage. Yet he kenned she was attracted to him, and enjoyed their conversation and banter. Neither could her passion in the bedchamber be faked. A conundrum to be sure.

"Aye, the lass is welcome to stay for a visit," Liam said. "I know my wife was looking forward to spending time with her sister." He looked affectionately at Sybil.

"In that case, I best be on my way." Braeden stood and held out his hand. "Walk with me to the door, love."

He took her hand as they made their way to the entrance hall. He felt as if leaving her here would somehow put a wedge between them that could prove insurmountable. On the other hand, insisting she go with him when her journey had been for the intention of spending time with her sister and the new bairns seemed cruel. He just wished she didn't seem so happy to see him leave.

They walked into the scant sunlight and down the pathway. Braeden turned and rested his hands on her shoulders. "As I told ye before, I keep a room at Dundas for my use when I'm not at university. If my time here is longer than I hope it will be, I will secure a house for us to live in until I receive word about my expedition."

She bit her lower lip and gave him a small smile. When she didn't speak, he added, "I hope ye enjoy the visit with yer sister and her bairns. I will let ye know when the letter from the committee on the expedition to Rome arrives."

"What will we do then?"

He didn't know, so he said, "I will decide when the time comes."

"*You* will decide?"

"'Tis my work that we're discussing here, lass. 'Tis verra important." He should have bitten his tongue. Sarah's eyes flashed, and her shoulders stiffened. Before she could lash out at him, he leaned forward and took her mouth in a gentle kiss. "Dinna fash yerself, lass. Have a good time with yer sister."

Tapping her lightly on the end of her nose, he turned and walked away.

"Are you walking to Dundas?" Her voice sounded bleak to his ears, but that must have been his imagination. Or wishful thinking.

He turned around but continued to walk backward. "Aye. 'Tis only about a two hour walk. 'Twill give my muscles some exercise after all that travel."

She wrapped her arms around her waist and nodded. With a small salute, he turned and never looked back until he passed the rise where he knew he could no longer see Bedlay. Then he let out a huge breath.

Dear Sarah,

When I arrived home there was a letter from the Royal Society of Edinburgh. A second candidate has been nominated for the Rome archeological position, so they have asked me to be patient while they research the man's background. In the meantime, I have a number of things I am taking care of while I have the time.

I miss your laughter and our conversations. Once again I am reminded of how different I am from the rest of my family.

I hope all is well with you and your family. Braeden

Sarah sat rocking Andrina as the babe fussed. The poor little mite seemed to be having difficulties with her tummy. She would draw her tiny legs up and howl. Sybil had tried walking and then rocking her, but Sarah offered to take over when the new mother looked as if she were about to drop.

Lady MacBride and the girls had gone to the village, leaving only the nurse who was busy with Donald wailing his own misery. It amazed Sarah how much time dealing with a little babe took and how many hands were needed when there were two of them.

Three days had passed since Braeden had returned to Dundas. During that time she'd missed him so much it hurt. She couldn't help but wonder how receptive he would be to her plan to return to London while he traveled to Rome. But her work was just as important to her as Braeden's was to him.

Perhaps she should have told him about her book, but she was afraid he would laugh and dismiss her dreams. His scorn would hurt more than anything he could say. That she wanted his approval annoyed her; but the fact of the matter was, she did. She had a great deal of respect for the man, and she didn't want to see laughter in his eyes at something that meant so much to her.

For now, it was best to keep it to herself. Even if he didn't laugh, she doubted he would understand her need to gain recognition for her hard work. Why did men have to be so male?

Thinking of his very male hands on her body and how he brought such pleasure to her with those hands and his mouth had her squirming in her chair. It was extremely annoying that he'd left her with those memories. And desires. Life would have been much simpler had she not met the man. She could have had a fulfilling life without all that passion. One could not miss what one never experienced.

"Hey sweetheart, it looks like your troubles have passed." Sarah gazed at her niece, who had settled down, her eyes slowly closing, her lips moving as if feeding. A sense of peace descended on the sitting room outside of the laird's bedchamber, where Sybil had gone to rest.

"Now that you're nice and quiet, maybe your mama can sleep. You and your brother are wearing her out."

Sarah continued to rock, the babe falling into a peaceful slumber. The child was soft and warm and smelled as only a new baby smelled. How wonderful it would be to hold her own child.

She quickly pushed that thought from her mind. Motherhood was not part of her plan. In order to have a child, she needed a husband, and the one she had she was trying her best to avoid.

Dear Braeden,

The babes seem to grow more each day. Lady MacBride and I try to do as much as we can for

Sybil, and Liam is very helpful as well. I went for a long walk yesterday and found a four-leaf clover. Isn't that supposed to bring good luck?

The beautiful countryside reminded me how much I enjoy picnics. We've never gone on a picnic.
Sarah

Braeden closed the thick book and pinched the bridge of his nose. He looked around Duncan's library where he'd been ensconced for two days. He spent too much time with his head buried in a book, behind closed doors. After a lifetime of that, it amused him that now he felt the pull of the outdoors. Perhaps Sarah's note had prompted the new feeling.

True, he and the lass hadn't gone on a picnic. They also hadn't done anything young couples do when they are courting. Maybe she would be more comfortable with their wedded state if he made an effort to woo her.

He grew excited at the idea of a picnic, as well as seeing Sarah again. He'd loved talking to her. Due to her education, she thought more along the lines he did. His parents had attempted to make him feel like part of the family, but the divide between them was even wider since he'd gone off to university.

Perhaps if he fetched her from Bedlay and even managed to make love to her on the soft grass, she might remember she was a married woman and belonged with her husband. Although his family hadn't said anything, it was obvious from their vague comments that they thought the separation of a newly married couple odd. But they'd always thought he was odd, anyway.

"There he is, always reading." His eldest brother Morgan entered the library, tugging off his work gloves. "Yer head is going to explode with all that knowledge in there, lad."

"Aye, there are times I believe 'tis true."

Morgan rested his work-roughened hands on his hips. "I have a way for ye to get some exercise for yer body instead of yer head."

"What?"

"I have a few sheep I need to chase down, and I could use another hand. They wandered through a hole in the fence and scattered. My boys are with the rest of the flock on the southeast pasture. And with Moira in a family way again, I can't ask her to help out."

Morgan kept his wife, Moira "in a family way" on a regular basis. At only thirty-four years, Morgan was already father to six bairns. With another on the way.

"Aye, I think I could use a bit of exercise." Braeden placed the book on a small table next to him and followed his brother.

> *Dear Sarah,*
>
> *Aye, 'tis a shame we've never gone on a picnic. I spent time with my brother, Morgan, rounding up sheep yesterday and realized I need more time outdoors. The fresh air cleared the cobwebs in my brain.*
>
> *I will be calling at Bedlay Castle Thursday next to escort you to a favorite spot of mine for a picnic.*
>
> *Wear clothes in which you feel comfortable climbing a tree. I will supply the food.*
>
> *Braeden*

Sarah rose from her bed filled with anticipation. Braeden was coming this morning to take her on a picnic. She shouldn't be so eager. The idea of them living apart was to allow her time to enjoy her niece and nephew and wait for word from her publisher, without risking a chance of Braeden's lovemaking causing her to increase.

Three weeks had passed since they'd had their second wedding. During that time she'd gotten to know her little niece and nephew and caught up on all her correspondence with those at home. She'd also finished her second book and was quite happy with the result.

Frankly, now she was a bit bored, but had a hard enough time admitting it to herself, without sharing that information with her sister, since Sybil believed the babes were the most interesting creatures on earth.

Sybil was so wrapped up in motherhood and running Bedlay that her time with Sarah was scant. Watching Liam and Sybil cast glances at each other in the special way lovers do bothered her more than she'd expected. The slight touches when they passed or the twinkle in Liam's eyes when they retired early to their bedchamber had her squirming, wishing she were retiring to her bedchamber with Braeden.

Best to stop thinking along those lines.

She'd almost had herself convinced the malaise she suffered from was the change in her relationship with her twin. Truth be told, it had all vanished when she'd received Braeden's note. As she considered spending a lazy afternoon with him, lying about on a blanket in the sun, speaking of books, history, and other subjects they both enjoyed, her spirits had lifted in a surprising way.

Sarah tied the wide bonnet ribbon under her chin. Alice had just come to her room to inform her that Braeden had arrived. She assured her there was no hurry since Liam had invited him into the library, and they were holed up in there.

She smoothed her gown, smirking at the outfit she wore underneath. Braeden had said to wear clothes comfortable while climbing trees, and she had. Her breeches and shirt had been specially made by a very closed-mouth dressmaker, who had duplicated the ensemble for all her sisters as well. Except Marion. Her lofty eldest sister never wore breeches.

The Lacey girls rode hard, and their father insisted they wear breeches while at their country estate so they didn't have to ride sidesaddle. It had been many years since Sarah had climbed a tree, but on a dare, she just might do that. One final glimpse of her ladylike appearance and she left the room.

Liam and Braeden were leaving the library as she reached the bottom step in the entrance hall. Her breath caught at the first sight of her husband in more than three weeks. Had he always been so handsome? So imposing?

No one who spent his entire life doing research, teaching, and reading should have those muscles. Despite Liam's immense size, Braeden stood shoulder to shoulder with her brother-in-law. Maybe not as massive, but certainly impressive enough.

"Ah, there ye are, lass." Braeden walked toward her, a genuine smile on his face. Her heart promptly skittered around her chest before settling down into a series of loud thumps. The deep resonance of his voice, the warm touch of his hand on hers, and she was ready to invite him up to her bedchamber and forget the picnic.

Luckily her cool head prevailed, and she merely smiled and allowed him to wrap his arms around her and kiss her senseless. Which no doubt would have continued for some time except for Liam clearing this throat.

Braeden pulled back, fortunately still holding onto her or she would have sunk to the floor in a puddle. "Are ye ready for our picnic?"

"Yes." Good heavens, was that her voice? She cleared her throat and smoothed back the nonexistent hair from her forehead. "I am ready."

Braeden extended his elbow, and she took his arm. "The picnic basket is in the carriage. Duncan's cook fixed a fine meal for us."

"Enjoy yerselves," Liam said. "Sarah has been working hard helping Sybil. She needs a restful afternoon."

With a twinkle in his eye, Braeden studied her from under shuttered eyelids. "Aye, restful, indeed."

Chapter Fourteen

When the sun made an appearance in the Highlands it was truly a magnificent thing. The green was so brilliant it almost hurt Braeden's eyes. 'Twas hard to admit, since the sight of his wife as she descended the stairs had done quite a bit to his eyesight as well.

The lass was just as lovely as he'd remembered. No one affected him like she did, even her identical twin sister. 'Twas something special about his Sarah that called to him. The sisters could stand side by side dressed the same and he'd know his wife. As he was sure Liam would know Sybil.

Braeden drove the carriage himself since he preferred not to have an audience if he was able to seduce Sarah. If she guessed his intention, she didn't show it, just seemed to enjoy the ride and the fresh air.

"How are the bairns?"

"They are so sweet." She grinned. "For a few days they had some stomach upset which kept us all from sleeping. A midwife from the village gave Sybil a tisane for the babies to drink, and that eased them somewhat. They are doing just fine now, and we are all sleeping peacefully."

"I would think with Liam, Sybil, Lady MacBride, Catriona, Alanna, ye, and however many servants work in the castle, dealing with the bairns would not be a strain."

"Sybil and I come from an unusual family, given our ducal status. My mother relied very little on nurses and nannies. We had governesses, to be sure, but everyone knew Mother was in charge. Any woman employed to deal with the children was under strict orders to summon my mother should any sort of a problem arise. It appears to me that Sybil is doing her best to follow in Mother's footsteps."

"And ye? Do ye expect to deal with yer own bairns as well?"

Her head snapped up, and she regarded him. He continued to stare at the road. "If a babe does present itself, I assume that would be true."

"I would like that," he said.

"What? A babe or not relying on others?"

He glanced at her. "Both." The thought of Sarah's body swelling with his bairn did something strange to his insides. What if they did conceive a child? That was something he'd have to think about for the future. Leaving a wife and child behind while he traipsed around the world on expeditions would not be what he'd want for his life. Nor did he find dragging them along appealing.

On the other hand, he was too young to give up his dreams. He wanted the Rome expedition, and probably one after that, then another one. He would have to be careful, and begin using French letters. Somehow the thought of using those with his own wife made him uncomfortable. Though that would only be a problem if he was able to get his wife into his bed again.

He shook off his gloomy thoughts and rising frustration that oftentimes came when he considered his marriage and focused instead on the beautiful woman alongside him and the wonderful summer day. He pointed to the left. "Up over that hill is the spot I told ye about. When I was a lad I played there with my brothers and cousins. There is a small lake— well, actually more like a large pond—where I learned to swim. In winter it turns into a fine ice skating pond."

"How exciting! My brother and sisters and I love ice skating. Mother took us to a place in the village where we skated with other children. When we returned home Cook would spoil us with her special cinnamon buns and hot chocolate. I never eat a cinnamon bun that I don't think of those times."

"It sounds as though ye had a wonderful childhood."

"Yes. I did."

"Tell me about yer da."

She smiled softly. "He was a wonderful father. I still have a hard time speaking of him."

"How did he die?"

She took a deep breath and stared off into the distance. "He was thrown from his horse. Broken neck."

"*Ach*, lass. 'Tis verra sorry I am for ye and yer family. It must have been a difficult time."

She nodded, tears standing in her eyes. "I was with my mother all night after we received word of his death." 'Twas obvious the loss of her da had affected her deeply. However, he didn't bring her on a picnic to drag out unpleasant memories and upset her. "I told ye to wear clothes ye could climb a tree in."

Blinking rapidly to clear her eyes, she tilted her mouth in a half smile. "I did." When his brows drew together, she laughed. "You will just have to wait and see."

Braeden shifted the reins to his right hand and grasped Sarah's hand. So soft and small compared to his. Everything protective in him arose, wanting to assure her he would take care of her for the rest of her life. If only she would reconcile herself to their marriage, he knew they would do well together.

He was certainly not rich and could not provide her with the sort of life she'd had growing up as the daughter of a duke. But he'd made some good decisions, and invested most of his salary from the university, so he had a tidy sum. Certainly enough to buy them a decent house when they settled somewhere along with securing enough staff to run it.

Once he received her dowry, he would invest that also for the benefit of their children. But most of all, he wanted to wrap his arms around her and assure her he would always be there for her and provide her with a good life. Home and family. That would also be important to Sarah. She grew up in a large, loving family that she would surely want for herself.

Yet, if he dragged her away from her family to his expedition in Rome, wouldn't that cause her pain? His lips tightened. His work had to come first, and he needed to remember that.

He drew the carriage to a stop. "Here we are. Let's enjoy a pleasant afternoon. Ye have been working hard, and could use the rest."

Dear Braeden,

Thank you so much for the wonderful picnic. Needless to say Alice was distressed to find that my gown had been sacrificed to the lake. I tried to explain to her that it was worth it to view all the McKinnon land from the top of your favorite tree. Who knew the wind would kick up just then and blow my gown into the water?

I'm sorry our time was cut short by the rainstorm that followed. Hopefully, you did not catch a chill. Alice fixed me a hot drink and tucked me right into bed.

Sarah

A week after the picnic, Sarah once again donned her breeches and shirt for a ride. She'd been spending a great deal of time with the babes and needed some fresh air. Truth be known, her stay with Sybil was becoming strained. Something she would never have thought was possible with her twin. They'd never had problems between them before, but with the major changes in Sybil's life, it was not a surprise.

More likely the tension came from Liam's disapproval of her staying away from Braeden. No doubt when he and Sybil were alone, he urged her to send Sarah to her husband. A reasonable request, after all.

It had been more than a month since their wedding, and she expected any day to receive word from her publisher that he needed her in London. His message might even arrive before Braeden received word of the expedition. Then she could say good-bye, wish him well, and be off to London and the thrill of being recognized as a published author. Her life would be stimulating and rewarding.

Lonely and frustrating.

Where had that thought come from?

A ride would be just the thing to pull her from these disturbing thoughts and feelings. There was about another hour before she would have to change for dinner with the family and clan members, as was the practice at Bedlay.

The stableboy, Brian, had tacked Ambrose for her, the horse she'd been riding ever since she'd arrived. After a leg up from the boy, she left the area at a slow walk, then a trot, and finally a canter. The early evening air was cool and fresh as it blew through her hair, clearing the cobwebs from her brain.

As a child she had loved the country air more than the smells and closeness of London. For the last four years, once the Season had ended and her family had packed up to leave, she had welcomed waving good-bye to Town.

After about fifteen minutes of riding, she was close to where she and Braeden had spent the afternoon on a picnic. He had looked somewhat disappointed when the storm had broken. She had laughed when they climbed down from the tree and saw her gown floating on the small lake. Although he'd offered to wade into the water to collect the garment, she'd refused. The heavy rainfall had them scrambling to gather up the picnic things and racing toward the carriage.

They'd arrived at the vehicle laughing and out of breath, water sluicing from their bodies. By the time they'd reached Bedlay, she was shivering with the cold, goose bumps covering her body. Braeden walked her to the door, kissed her in a way that chased away the chill, then turned and left her there. A slight feeling of abandonment had filled her as she watched him run to the carriage and jump inside.

Keeping Ambrose at a steady trot, she rounded the lake as she ruminated on all that had happened to her since she'd left England to visit her sister. Who would have thought she'd end up married? She'd certainly been privy to the stories of couples who had run off to Gretna Green. With that knowledge, she should have been more aware of what she was doing when she declared them married in front of witnesses.

All these thoughts ran through her head as she turned from where they'd had their picnic and started toward home. But it wasn't home, was it? Not hers, anyway. She sighed. All of this deliberating was giving her a headache.

From the side of her eye she caught sight of a small animal darting out, running right in front of her horse. Spooked, Ambrose let out with a screeching neigh and reared back, catching Sarah completely unprepared.

She fought to hold her seat, but the force of the animal's movement threw her backward, and she tumbled onto the ground, landing flat on her back, her head smacking on something very hard.

Braeden tore his attention away from his book on Ancient Rome as Duncan opened the library door and entered. His face was pale, his lips tight.

"What's wrong, Laird?" Braeden closed the heavy book in his lap and set it aside. For some unknown reason, his heartbeat sped up.

"Word just came from Bedlay. Sarah was thrown from a

horse and is unconscious."

Before Duncan could say any more, Braeden was out of the chair and headed to the door.

"I sent instructions to the stable lad to have a horse prepared for ye," Duncan shouted as Braeden exited.

"Thank ye." He jogged the length of the corridor and grabbed his coat from the hook by the main door.

Thrown from a horse. Just the other day Sarah had told him the story of her da dying from a fall. Broken neck, she'd said. His stomach muscles tightened at the thought of Sarah lying pale and still, her lively spirit gone from this world. He'd been in such a rush he never even thought to ask Duncan if any other information had been sent.

Even though he was anxious to get to the castle, once he was mounted, he had to pick his way carefully with scant moonlight to show the way. From the distance he could see Bedlay, lit from inside, like a beacon. His heartbeat picked up as the castle drew near. Hopefully, the lass had awakened by now.

He swung his leg over the horse and threw the reins in the direction of the stable lad. The front door opened before he was able to sound the knocker. Liam greeted him with a curt nod. "This way."

They proceeded up the stairs, then made a right turn to the room he remembered as Sarah's. "Is she still unconscious?"

"Aye." Liam ran his fingers through his hair. "The village healer's been to see her. She said with these head injuries, only time will tell. Sarah apparently struck her head on a rock, which knocked her out." The laird pushed open the door. Braeden's breath hitched at the sight. Sarah lay perfectly still on the large bed in the center of the room.

Sybil sat by her side, reading from a book.

She put the tome down and stood as the men entered. "How is she?" Braeden asked.

"The same." She touched his arm. "The healer said nothing seems to be broken. She had a gash on the back of her head, and there was blood on a rock that she must have struck."

Braeden approached the bed and sat alongside Sarah on the mattress. He pushed back the few strands of hair from her forehead. "How did the accident happen?"

Sybil wrapped her arms around her middle. "Sarah went for a ride by herself late this afternoon. When she didn't return in time for dinner, Liam went in search of her. He found her lying on the ground, the horse she was riding nearby, almost as if he was watching over her.

"He brought her home on his horse. The healer was sent for, and she said we need to give her body time to come around."

Braeden took her cool hand in his. Amazing how lovely she looked even in repose. There was a slight tint to her cheeks, her lips a ruby red, and she appeared to be merely asleep. But he knew, from the McKinnon healer whom he'd followed around when he'd been a lad, that one could easily slip from a coma into death.

"I will stay here with her tonight. Ye look tired, Sybil." Braeden turned to Liam. "You should take yer wife to bed. She looks about to collapse."

"Aye. The mon has the right of it, Sybil. Ye need yer rest to take care of Sarah and the bairns." Liam held out his hand.

She rose, placed her hand on Braeden's shoulder, and gave him a comforting squeeze. "I will see her in the morning."

"Thank ye." His attention remained riveted on his wife as Liam and Sybil took their leave.

A cheery fire burned in the fireplace, but he felt chilled to the bone. He moved to the chair Sybil had occupied and slumped, his long legs stretched before him, watching Sarah as her chest moved up and down. At least she was alive.

As frightened as he was at the fall she'd taken, when she woke up, he would kiss her soundly and then order her to have her maid pack her belongings and move to Dundas. No more staying with her sister. She belonged with him, and all this nonsense of her staying at Bedlay while he lived alone would end.

"Get better, lass, because I ken ye will try to dissuade me. But not this time."

Chapter Fifteen

"Braeden?" Sarah's raspy voice jarred him from the light doze he'd been slipping in and out of all night. He ran his hand down his face and sat up. "Sarah. Thank God yer awake."

"What are you doing here? And why does my head hurt so much?"

Braeden climbed from the uncomfortable chair and stretched his back muscles, then moved to ease himself down on the bed. "Ye were thrown from yer horse and struck yer head. Liam went in search of ye when ye never returned for dinner last night and brought ye back. Then they sent for me." He took her hand in his. "Ye had us all quite worried."

"What time is it?"

Braeden glanced out the window. "Just after dawn."

"Have you been here all night?"

"And where else would I be?" Realizing his manner was much too gruff for a lass who just woke up from a head injury, he softened his voice. "Aye, I've been right here all night." He touched her cheek. "And 'tis verra happy I am that yer awake."

A slight knock on the door drew their attention. Sybil entered, a bright smile on her face. "I thought I heard voices and assumed you were awake. How do you feel?"

"Horrible. With a very large headache."

Sybil moved closer to the bed. "The healer said it would take a few days before you feel better. But she also said you didn't break any bones."

Braeden closed his eyes. "Thank God for that."

"Do you feel up to some tea?" Sybil asked.

"Yes." Sarah tried to ease her body up, then dropped back with a wince. "That would be nice."

"Stay still, lass. 'Twill not help yer head any to be moving about."

"The healer left a tisane for you to take that will ease the pain in your head." Sybil headed to the door. "I'll bring it when I return with the tea."

As soon as Sybil left the room, Braeden took Sarah's hands in his. It seemed that was all the lass needed to turn into a watering pot. Tears slowly dripped down her cheeks. "I was so frightened when the horse reared up. All I could think about was my father breaking his neck."

"Aye. I'm sure you did." He reached out and touched her damp cheek. 'Twas time to let the lass know her stay here at Bedlay had come to an end. For whatever reason, it was obvious Sarah did not accept their marriage, would not accept him, and was playing some type of childish game. Well, it would all end now. Even if their marriage had been unplanned and perhaps not to her liking, the fact remained:

they were married and it was time for her to acknowledge that.

Sarah wiped her face and gave him a hint of a smile. "I probably shouldn't cry. It only makes my head hurt more."

"Once yer feeling up to it, ye will travel with me to Dundas." He failed to make the statement come out softer than it did.

"What do you mean?"

"'Tis simple, lass. This hiding with yer sister, pretending yer still a single lass, must come to an end. Ye've had a visit with Sybil, ye've enjoyed her bairns, but now 'tis time to acknowledge that yer a married woman, and yer place is with yer husband."

He could have bitten his tongue when her face paled even further. He'd promised himself he would give her time to recover, and here he was ordering her about and making things worse barely ten minutes after the lass had woken up. "*Ach*, lass. I'm sorry to upset ye."

Before Sarah could respond, Sybil returned to the room carrying a tray with a teapot, several cups, and a plate of baked goods. "Mrs. MacDougal sent some fresh cakes and bread for you."

Braeden helped Sarah sit up, and Sybil placed the tray across her lap.

"I brought the tisane to ease the ache in your head." Sybil snapped open a napkin and handed it to her sister. "Mrs. MacDougal sent enough for the three of us, so why don't we all have a bit of breakfast?"

Sybil made quick work of pouring and fixing everyone's tea and passing the plate of bread and cakes. Perhaps sensing the tension in the room, she made small talk about her bairns and how Liam was becoming adept at changing nappies.

Once they'd all had their fill, Sybil removed the tray. "I'll send Alice in to help you wash. I think you should get as much sleep as you can today. It will help the healing."

Braeden stood and kissed Sarah lightly on the forehead. "There are a few matters I need to see to today, lass, to prepare for your arrival tomorrow." He turned to Sybil. "Please have Alice pack Sarah's belongings. She's moving to Dundas with me."

Sybil nodded. "Of course." She darted a glance at Sarah. "I think that is best. I'll take care of all that while you recover."

Sarah wanted to scream with frustration. She hated everyone planning things for her and talking over her as if she weren't even present. And since when did Braeden become so overbearing? In one breath he told her she was moving to his room at Dundas, and before they even had a chance to discuss it, he ordered Sybil to have Alice pack her belongings.

All the goings-on only increased the pain in her head. What she wanted more than anything right now was the tisane Sybil had given her to take effect and more sleep. She didn't want to think about her interfering husband or her obliging sister.

Sybil and Braeden walked to the door, their heads together as they spoke. Most likely arranging the rest of her life. Sarah shifted on the bed and faced the window so she wouldn't have to watch them. Soon the tisane would help her sleep—her last thought before she drifted into darkness.

Sarah awoke to bright sunlight streaming through the window facing the foot of her bed. Alice hummed as she folded gowns and placed them into her trunks.

She rose up on her elbows. "What are you doing?"

Alice turned to her, a huge smile on her face. "I'm packing your clothes. Did you have a nice nap?"

"Hardly a nap, I'm just trying to avoid pain," she mumbled. At least her head didn't hurt as much as it had when she'd awoken before. She eased her body back onto the pillow and sulked like an obstinate child. Her husband had ordered her to move to Dundas, and it seemed everyone was rather jolly with the idea except her. No one cared what she thought, what she wanted. Exactly why she'd decided to have an independent life. A life she chose, not one forced on her.

"Alice, can you ask Sybil to join me?"

The maid patted the gown she'd just put into the trunk. "Yes, my lady. I saw her a few moments ago, and she was going down to ask Mrs. MacDougal for a bit of soup for you."

Sarah closed her eyes and tried her best to block out the sounds of Alice succumbing to Braeden's edict. Was there no one on her side? Did she not have a say on where she would lay her head at night? Her eyes opened with a snap. Would Braeden expect her to sleep with him? And do other things that happened in a bed?

He'd mentioned he had a "room" at Dundas, so there was most likely no chance of her having a separate bed to sleep in. If only she could be sure she could stay strong and not succumb to his attentions. His kisses and caresses would most assuredly wear down her resistance. If she allowed Braeden to make love to her, there was a chance she could conceive a child, and there would go her dreams.

She must teach her traitorous body to behave itself. It was all so confusing, and her persistent headache didn't help sort out all the problems that lined up in her brain like soldiers on parade.

"Here we are. Mrs. MacDougal prepared wonderful cock-a-leekie soup for you." Sybil bustled into the room, once again carrying a heavily laden tray. One glance at Sarah's mulish expression and Sybil addressed Alice. "You can take time for your luncheon now. I'll sit with Sarah."

"Thank you, my lady." Alice finished laying a bright yellow scarf on top of the gowns in the trunk and left the room.

"What's the matter?" Sybil didn't wait long to go on the attack. She placed the tray on Sarah's lap and pulled up a chair alongside the bed.

"Why do you think there is anything the matter?"

"Has it slipped your mind that, as your twin, no one knows you better than I do? In fact, I know you so well, I can tell you what the matter is." Before Sarah had a chance to answer, Sybil continued, "You are annoyed that Braeden ordered you to pack up and go to his home."

"How dare he just come in here, command my maid to pack my belongings, and then stroll out of here without so much as a bye-your-leave? Who does he think he is?"

"Your husband." Sybil raised her hand as Sarah opened her mouth to speak. "And it is time. He's been very patient, you know."

Sarah raised her chin, wincing as her head throbbed at the movement. "I can assure you I have no idea what you're talking about."

"Of course you do. Stop being silly. You've been married for more than a month, and you have yet to share a residence with your husband. How long did you think he would allow that?"

"Need I remind you, I was coming here and endured that blasted journey for the sole purpose of visiting *you*, not to marry some man on the road?"

"Oh, Sarah," Sybil said, smiling and shaking her head. "Aside from the fact that it was your mistake that married the two of you, it is very obvious to me that you care for Braeden, as he does for you."

"No." Sarah struggled to sit up. "I do not care for him. At least, not the way one cares for a husband. I can't do that. I won't do that."

"Who are you?" Sybil strung the words out. "You're giving me the impression you purposely don't want to have feelings for your husband. I know you remember our late night conversations about how we all wanted love in our marriages, not the typical *ton* alliances. Isn't that what we all planned to hold out for? You, me, Abigail, Marion, Mary?"

Sybil snapped open the napkin and tucked it under Sarah's chin. "I'm quite sure you still haven't told Braeden about your book." She picked up the spoon, dipped it into the soup, and pointed it at Sarah's face.

Frowning, Sarah took the spoon from her sister's hand. "I can certainly feed myself."

"Well?" Sybil said. "Have you told him?"

"No."

"Why not?"

Sarah sighed and wiped her mouth. "I truly don't think he would understand, and what difference would it make anyway? He is planning on going to Rome, and I have to be in London. That means we cannot be together, anyway."

"If you talk to him, maybe the two of you can come to a compromise."

"You well know any compromise will be on my part. Men don't concede, they make their wives adhere to their wishes."

Sybil studied her, and Sarah looked away. She couldn't explain how very much this meant to her. How could she tell her beloved twin sister that always being one half of a pair had sometimes left her frustrated? Years of sharing everything from birthdays, to identical gifts, to friends, to their come-out balls. Her writing was something that belonged to her, alone. It wasn't something she had to share with Sybil.

Now because of the rash words she had spouted out in some unknown inn in Scotland, she was married to Braeden. She was going to be part of a pair again—just when she'd worked so hard to be independent.

"This is the cottage you've been living in?" Sarah stared out the carriage window at the impressive stone building about a mile down the pathway from Dundas Castle. The vehicle carrying them to her new residence had just rolled to a stop.

"Nay. I keep a room at Dundas for when I'm not at my house in Edinburgh, but when Duncan learned ye were finally joining me, he offered the use of the cottage while we're still in Scotland. I had yer things delivered this morning, and I believe ye will be comfortable for as long as we need to stay here."

She pushed away his last comment. Right now, her head ached and she was much too tired to begin the conversation about her book, and what that meant.

"Where do your parents live?"

Braeden pointed west of where the stone cottage sat. "Mum and Da live over that hill, in a smaller place, since they work at the castle and are there all day. All my brothers and sisters have cottages scattered around them. My brothers and brothers-in-law breed sheep, and each have a small garden for their own use. They are fortunate to have kept their land. 'Tis a good life for them."

"But not the life for you."

"Nay."

It was three days after she'd been thrown from the horse. Her head pain had lessened to a mild throb. Despite her initial grumbling about Braeden dragging her from Bedlay, she was not unhappy about leaving Liam's home.

They'd all been very gracious to her, but she had begun to feel out of place. Lady MacBride and her daughters kept themselves busy with the running of the castle while Sybil and the nanny concerned themselves with the babes. They'd enjoyed having Sarah join them in the nursery, but she was certainly not needed there.

Liam spent hours each day dealing with estate matters. Last evening he and Sybil had made a visit to her bedchamber.

Liam thanked her for visiting and made a point of telling her it was proper for her to take her place alongside her husband. And she would always be welcome at Bedlay.

For a visit, he'd added.

Braeden hopped down and strode to her side of the carriage. She held out her hand for him to assist her, but instead he gathered her into his arms and headed to the door. A servant opened the portal, and they sailed through.

Being this close to Braeden for the first time in weeks did something to her insides. The familiar warmth of his body, the scent of his soap, the strength of his arms holding her, enveloped her with a sense of safety and protection. She must learn to control those feelings. It wasn't something she wanted to get comfortable with. They would soon be parting ways, he to his work, she to hers.

She glanced at his strong features, his determined jaw, high cheekbones, and deep blue eyes behind rounded spectacles. Her lady parts fluttered, reminding her that allowing Braeden to make love to her could end with a babe on the way. Perhaps she could use her head injury as an excuse to avoid his attentions, but eventually that would end, and Braeden would be very persistent in his desire for her.

"Do ye want to rest in bed for a while?"

"No. Please, I'm tired of bed. Is there a sitting room? And can you please put me down? I can certainly walk." She had to set some distance between them, even though all she wanted to do was burrow into his warm safe body and never face another day with the questions and confusion she'd been dealing with for weeks.

"Ye will walk once I get ye settled. I won't have ye falling because you're weak."

She gasped. "I am not weak!"

Ignoring her protest, he continued down the corridor and made a turn into a brightly lit room.

She gasped. "Oh, this is lovely." The pale rose and green room had obviously been decorated by a woman. One with very good taste. An Aubusson carpet of a Renaissance floral print covered the entire area. Three comfortable chairs surrounded a small table in the center of the room with a bowl of fresh flowers.

Large windows with deep green floral drapes allowed the afternoon sun to cast dappled shadows from a large oak tree a few feet from the cottage. Along the mantelpiece, small carved wooden animals kept watch from their perch.

Braeden deposited her on the settee near the brightly burning fireplace, which took some of the Scottish dampness from the air. Once she was settled, he drew up one of the chairs from the center of the room and sat, resting one booted foot over his knee.

He crossed his arms over his chest, looking like the professor he was. "I dinna ken how long this will be our home, but I want ye to feel comfortable here. We will continue to take our meals at Dundas, which I think ye will enjoy since yer friend Lady Margaret is looking forward to seeing ye."

She studied Braeden as he described the layout of the cottage and his plans for them to visit with his parents when she felt up to it. "They want to ken their daughter-in-law a bit better."

While he was talking, her thoughts wandered to how she could possibly spend time with him without losing her heart. His familiar face, expressive as he spoke, his spectacles slipping slightly down his nose that he pushed back automatically, and his little boy smile when he said something that pleased him, scared her to death.

She needed to continue to remind herself that her life was not with this man, but in London. Even though it startled her to realize the joyful notion of an independent life had faded a bit. Once he'd carried her in his arms, she knew he already owned a part of her heart.

Chapter Sixteen

Later that evening, Braeden and Sarah took the short ride back to the cottage after supping with Duncan and members of his clan in the great hall. Sarah would have preferred to walk, but in the end she was glad for Braeden's insistence that they ride. On the way back, her head began to pound, bringing on a slight nausea.

She entered the cottage on Braeden's arm, a slight moan escaping from her lips as a sharp pain stabbed her head.

"Are ye all right?" He eyed her with concern.

"Actually, I believe I would like to retire. I'm having some pain and could use a bit of that tisane the healer sent home with me."

"Aye, I'll summon Alice to help ye." Again he scooped her into his arms, but instead of resenting the action, she snuggled closer and inhaled his comforting smell. The constant pain in her head was wearing her out. She didn't have the strength or desire to fight her feelings right now.

Once he laid her gently on the bed, he left with a promise to send Alice in and to return to sit with her for a while before she slept. Closing her eyes, she took deep breaths and tried to relax. When her mind was wrestling with her fears and concerns, the pain grew worse.

It had been pleasant seeing Lady Margaret again. Actually, her friend was now Lady McKinnon since she'd married the laird. It had been her wedding that brought Sybil to the Highlands. Sarah had intended to come, as well, but ague had kept her from the trip.

No one in their family had much to do with the Highlands, yet both she and her twin had ended up married to Scottish men. Sarah's idea of Highlanders had been men who fought, swilled whiskey, and chased women. That notion had been disabused after she'd met Liam when he had arrived at their home in Manchester Manor to convince Sybil to marry him. True love. Something she was avoiding like the plague.

Maybe it's too late?

Although Liam had changed Sarah's opinion of the Highlanders, nothing had prepared her for a man such as Braeden McKinnon, Scottish or not. She continued to marvel at his intelligence and having secured a university position at such a young age. Unfortunately, there were too many things about this unintentional husband of hers that she admired.

"My lady, are you feeling a bit of pain?" Alice bustled into the room.

"Yes." Sarah straightened and eased off the bed. "Please help me undress and prepare for sleep. And I would love a sip of the tisane to ease the pain somewhat."

"This is a lovely house that Mr. McKinnon has." Alice

folded the gown she'd removed from Sarah. "Will you be living here permanently?"

"No. Laird McKinnon has let this house to Mr. McKinnon while he awaits his letter from the Royal Society of Edinburgh about the expedition he hopes to join. After he receives that..." She shrugged.

Alice stripped her down to her underclothes and helped her wash and dress in a warm, soft nightgown. After she was settled into bed and sipping on the warm liquid, Braeden stuck his head in the partially open door. "Are ye up for visitors, lass?"

Her maid gathered up the dirty clothes and made a quick exit. Sarah waved Braeden in and placed the cup of tisane on the table near her bed. The tingle in her stomach that spread upward toward her face had nothing to do with the tisane. It had everything to do with the man who settled himself in the chair near her bed, his long legs stretched out, crossed at the ankles.

Her husband. The man she'd pledged her life to, all legal and final after accidentally marrying them in front of an innkeeper. He rested his hand on his thigh, his fingers tapping a cadence to a song only he could hear. She licked her lips as she remembered how those hands and fingers had pleasured her. His slow smile told her he probably knew her thoughts, which produced a wave of heat that started low in her belly and spread to her face.

Conversation. That would be the best thing to distract her from the direction her thoughts were sprinting toward. "I met your parents and others in your family at our wedding, but I didn't have a chance to really speak with them. They seemed very pleasant."

"And anxious to ken more about their daughter-in-law," he said drily.

She squirmed at this slight admonishment. "You are so very different from your other family members. What was it like growing up with them?"

He leaned back and linked his fingers behind his head. "I think there were many times my mum and da dinna know what to make of me. My oldest sister, Fiona, was sickly most of her childhood, so Mum charged her with watching over me while she did her chores. Since Fiona loved to read, she read to me a great deal. I was only a bairn of about three when I started reading to her." He shrugged at her expression. "'Twas easy for me to pick up how to read from watching her.

"I started helping da with the figuring he did for the sheep business a couple of years later. He was a bit surprised when I caught several of his mistakes." He grinned, looking much like the young boy he must have been.

"That must have been a bit disconcerting for your parents."

"Aye. Luckily for me, despite being a sheep farmer, my da was a firm believer in education. Although my brothers and sisters only had schooling until they were able to read, write, and figure, he hired a tutor to continue with me."

"That was very forward-thinking of him."

"But I still had my chores to perform. That, he wasn't so forward-thinking about. I would rise before everyone else to get them finished so I could spend as much time as possible with my books. Once I opened the book cover, I was lost in a world of my own making."

"It sounds rather lonely." The image of a small boy, spectacles perched on his small nose, lost in his books while others his age played and worked alongside brothers and sisters twisted something inside.

"Not at all. I had my cousins. After a while Mum made me put the books down and go off with Ronson, my closest friend. He's my cousin also, and we have the distinction of being born the same day. Our mums are sisters."

Sarah took another sip of the tisane. Either the warming liquid or the conversation was distracting her enough that the pain had eased. "Then you almost have a twin, too."

"Aye, I guess you could say that. When we were bairns, our mums kept us together so Fiona could watch over us both."

"Where is Ronson now?"

"He married a lass from the Lowlands, and since she was her parents' only child, he agreed to live with her clan."

"He sounds like a nice person."

"Aye, he is nice, but he also had nothing left here. Ronson's two brothers headed to America years ago, and his parents died when their cottage burned to the ground. 'Twas right around the time he met Nora and immediately lost his heart to the lass. 'Twasn't much of a decision to agree to her parents' request for him to take their clan name. They married only two weeks after they met."

"We broke their record."

Braeden grinned. "We did indeed, lass."

"I fail to see the humor in it." Honestly, did Braeden think this was all entertainment? They were married to each other for life. Something she hadn't wanted, and here she was, sitting across from a man who could very well thwart her dreams and plans. And there was nothing she could do about it.

"If ye can see the humor in it, 'twould not upset ye so. Ye might think I dinna ken how ye feel about this, but I do. What confuses me is why yer so against marriage. Or is it merely marriage to me that has ye so distressed?"

How to answer that question without hurting him yet have him realize she would not be the wife he surely wanted? She had plans and commitments that were very separate from his. Plans she had no intention of abandoning. Unfortunately, he deserved more. He deserved a wife who would appreciate all he had to offer as a husband. She opened her mouth to speak and burst into tears.

Without a word Braeden toed off his boots and climbed into the bed with her. Pulling her into his arms he leaned his chin on her head. "*Ach*, lass. 'Tis a hard time for ye. Yer in pain, and need some time to heal. I ken that."

Why did he have to be so nice? So damned nice. She didn't even feel bad for thinking such a nasty, inappropriate word. The way she was treating him, compared to how he treated her, brought even more tears.

Braeden eased back and looked down at her. "Darlin', I'm thinking ye need a good night's sleep."

She wiped her nose with the handkerchief he'd handed her. "I believe you're right." With the move from her sister's home, and her injuries, her emotions had been up and down all day. Hopefully, after a few more days she would begin to feel more like herself.

"Lie down and I'll rub yer back until ye fall asleep."

Sarah scooted down and rolled to her side, presenting him with her back. The tisane relaxed her, and eventually the soothing touch of his palm stroking her back had her drifting off to sleep.

Braeden grinned at the soft snores coming from his wife. Propped up on his elbow, he continued to draw circles on her back as he gazed out the window at the darkened night.

He shifted onto his back and linked his fingers under his head. There was something troubling the lass. Although he didn't consider himself a great lover, he'd had enough contact with the lasses to ken when one was attracted to him. And the draw between him and Sarah was strong. What he'd learned of her upbringing and character, she would not have allowed him to make love to her if she didn't have feelings for him.

The question remained, why was she purposely holding herself back? Was it possible there was a lad at home she was fond of? Had hoped to marry? But then he remembered the lass saying she never intended to marry, and would simply be a doting aunt to her siblings' bairns. Verra strange.

Feeling tired himself, his eyes drifted closed, and soon he was as sound asleep as his wife.

Chapter Seventeen

"I'm taking the lass on a trip. She had such a hard time on her journey here, I thought it would be nice to show her more of Scotland without all the concerns and disruptions of her previous trip." Braeden leaned his forearms on his mum's kitchen table and fiddled with his teacup.

"I thought ye were waiting for a letter from yer committee?" Mum asked.

"Aye. But I think the distraction would be good for Sarah. She spends a great deal of time writing in this journal of hers. She needs some fresh air and something to occupy her time besides the journal. 'Tis not natural for a high-spirited lass like my Sarah to be indoors all the time hunched over a pen and paper."

"Sounds to me like ye and yer wife are well suited. 'Twas many a day I chased ye away from yer books." His mother smiled warmly at him.

Every day Sarah asked if his letter had arrived, almost as if she would be glad to be rid of him. It seemed the more determined she was to push him away, the more resolved he was to get back his Sarah who he'd come to know on the journey to her sister.

He'd even spent an afternoon at Bedlay, clucking over the bairns, so he could talk to Sybil about her twin. She seemed surprised when he mentioned Sarah spending all her time writing.

Sybil had patted the back of the tiny bairn in her arms and said, "Do you not know what she is writing?"

"Nay. She said 'tis a journal, but the lass never goes anywhere or does anything to require all that recording."

Sybil had tightened her lips and shook her head. With a deep sigh, she suggested he ask her about her writing, but he had pushed that thought away. If the lass wanted to record every minute of her day on paper rather than doing the sort of activities that would inspire all that writing, it was her decision.

He'd spent a great deal of his time researching and making notes, so 'twas better than if he felt the need to entertain her all the time. His mind returned to where he sat at his mum's table. He stood and pushed his chair in. "If my letter comes while we're away, hold onto it for me. They've let me wait all this time, so they will have to wait a few days for my acceptance."

"Where are ye and the lass headed?" his mother asked.

"Inverness." He shrugged. "I ken it's a long trip, but there is much to do and see there. Sarah and I have a liking for history, and there is plenty of Scottish antiquity in that area. I hope to fill our days with tours, and then…" Realizing he was speaking to his mum, he stopped short. 'Twas best not to announce the plans he had to occupy their evenings.

Braeden took the half hour walk from his parent's house to the stone cottage. The walk in the warm morning air gave him time to contemplate the upcoming trip he'd planned. Sarah had not shown much enthusiasm when he'd presented her with the idea. She had just nodded and then returned to her blasted writing.

His frustration grew every day also over the lack of response from the committee on the expedition. The trip had been scheduled to begin in late September. Here it was already mid-July, and still no decision had been made. If selected, he would need at least two months to prepare, and now time was growing short. It would be his job to order equipment and draw up the numerous notes, sketches, lists, and diagrams the team would require.

All of that needed to be done in addition to his personal packing, and now with a wife to join him, she would want time to prepare herself, as well. He shook his head, wondering what it was a lady would take with her on a scientific expedition. Which brought him full circle to his concern about Sarah and her coolness toward him.

This trip would be a honeymoon of sorts. To his way of thinking, Sarah spending the first several weeks of their marriage with her sister had started their problems. Not that he thought he should have denied her the visit. It had been, after all, the reason for the lass's trip to begin with. He couldn't help but think if she hadn't been thrown from her horse she might have stayed established in Bedlay Castle until she grew old.

Best to put all of those thoughts behind him and enjoy

this trip. It would be a new start for them. If he was going to be a part of the expedition, he would need to concentrate on his work, and worrying about his wife would be quite a distraction. Feeling hopeful for the first time in weeks, he whistled softly as he approached the stone cottage where the woman who was constantly in the front of his mind was preparing for the trip.

D espite her reluctance to spend time alone with Braeden, Sarah was excited about the excursion to Inverness. Traveling to new places always enlivened her spirit. Braeden had assured her the road to Inverness was well traveled. She found that comforting since she didn't desire a repeat of her trip from England to Bedlay.

She and Alice had gone through her wardrobe to select clothing to pack. She'd sent for some of her things from Manchester Manor, and they'd arrived a few days ago. In some ways, pulling out gowns she hadn't seen in months seemed as though she'd acquired new clothing.

Along with her possessions was a note from Drake. While not exactly scolding her, the tone was cool enough that she knew he surmised what had happened on the trip to Bedlay. The only way he would have gotten that information would be from Liam. Curse her interfering brother-in-law. Or should she say, *her laird*?

Truth be told, Liam was indeed the oldest male in her family here, and without a doubt, Drake would have taken Liam to task if he hadn't insisted on a wedding after hearing she and Braeden had spent the night together.

: **Read Immediately**

or Back Pain

o: **Robt Bruce**

reach you regarding Your Eligibility For
nd Insurance Back Support System

Back Support System [verify by phone]
Approved By Medicare and Insurance:

d and Fitted Back Brace
y Medicare
y Tested
asive
of Customers Use This System
UR PAIN

66-526-4274

RELEASE CODE: 02700
CLAIM DEADLINE: July 8, 2016

SPECIAL NOTICE: Medicare and Insurance I[

DELIVER EXCLUSIVELY TO: Robt Bruce

CLAIMS DOCUMENT REGISTERED '

```
*******************AUTO*
264441D120622          79
Robt Bruce
35 Park St # 1
Brandon VT 05733-1121
```

Her mother also wrote to say she was preparing for a trip to the Highlands to see her new grandchildren and visit with her daughters. There was a terse note as well that it would be nice to meet her new son-in-law since Sarah had married rather quickly.

Sarah had cringed when she read Mother's words. The poor woman had had to hurry up Sybil's wedding because her sister was already increasing when she arrived back on Manchester Manor's doorstep. Once Liam came after her, the news of her condition became known, and a speedy wedding had been performed.

If she and Braeden were gone long enough on this trip, her mother might very well arrive in their absence. The thought teased the back of her mind that should Braeden's expedition approval come through, she could travel back to London with her mother.

"Sarah, are ye packed yet?" Braeden's voice pulled her from her musings. She turned to see him leaning against the doorframe of her bedroom, anticipation on his handsome face.

"Almost."

He pushed himself away from the door and strolled into the room. "By the saints, lass. How much are ye taking?" He spun in a slow circle surveying the trunks Alice was diligently packing.

"I need enough gowns for day and evening. I assume we'll be going to the theater and museums and other things?"

He moved behind her and wrapped his arms around her waist, leaning in close to whisper in her ear. "Ye dinna need much. I like ye best with nothing on at all."

The feel of his warm breath against her neck, and the

vision of what he'd said, let loose a swirl of heat to drift to her lower parts, spreading rapidly through her body to enflame her face. "*Shh*. Alice can hear you."

"Nay. She's busy packing." He gathered the tendrils of hair falling against her neck and kissed the exposed skin, brushing his lips back and forth. Mesmerized, her head dropped and she closed her eyes, enjoying the sensation.

"Should I tell her to leave off the packing because yer husband wants you to spend all yer time naked?" His warm breath against her ear sent shivers up her spine.

"Braeden!" She turned to face him. "Stop that."

"Why?" He rested his wrists on her shoulders and trailed his thumbs over her heated cheeks. "'Tis been a long time, lass. Yer leaving me in a bad way."

Yes, it had been a long time, and her body reminded her of what she'd been missing. His eyes roamed her face, looking her over seductively, then settled on her lips. His large hand cupped her cheeks, and his head descended. The anticipation was almost unbearable as he moved closer, his soft breath bathing her before his lips covered hers hungrily.

The feel of his lips, the touch of his tongue urging her to open to him, had her awash in sensation and need. His strong arm wrapped around the curve of her waist, pulling her to him. She slid her hands up his chest to encircle his neck, her fingers playing with the soft hair that hung over his neckcloth.

Every thought in her head fled as he swept into her mouth, touching all the parts that caused her to shiver. There was an intimacy to their kiss that hadn't been there before. Or had she merely forgotten the powerful hold this man had on her senses?

He released her mouth and scattered kisses along her jaw, the hollow of her neck, then up to her ear to tease and lightly bite, then soothe the sensitive skin there. His hands roamed her body, touching, caressing, kneading her flesh.

The sound of the bedroom door closing echoed in the recesses of her mind, telling her Alice had left the room. She should be embarrassed at what the maid had witnessed, but there was no room for awkwardness with the sensations washing over her from Braeden's expert mouth and hands.

The man was a master and played her body like a fine instrument. She had no idea how it had happened, but within minutes her gown was gone and her stays had been untied. He made short work of the rest of her garments, which quickly vanished, and she stood naked in his arms, her clothing pooling at her feet. The feel of her sensitive skin rubbing against the rough fabric of his jacket brought her to a new level of awareness. Of her need for him. For his touch.

"*Ach*, lass, I've missed ye so much. Ye've been driving me daft for weeks. I need ye in my arms, need to feel your warmth surrounding me."

Before she had processed all his words, he swept her into his arms and strode to the bed. Gently, he laid her down then removed his shirt and boots. "Yer so lovely it makes my hands itch to touch yer skin, to feel how ready ye are for me."

Unabashed at her nakedness, she raised her arms in invitation, wanting—indeed needing—to feel the weight of his body crushing hers.

Eating her up with his eyes, he said, "Darlin', I could stare at ye all night, but if I don't take care of this ache yer causing me, I fear I might very well explode." He came down on top of her, fisting her curls in his hands, taking her mouth with a vengeance, demanding her complete surrender and accepting no less. This was a Braeden she'd not seen before. There was desperation in his touch, as though he needed to meld their bodies into one. As though he strived to have her lose herself in him.

Deft fingers stroked her heated center, circling her pearl as he whispered words of Gaelic in her ear. She writhed and moaned at his ministrations, moving her hand down to fist his hardened male flesh.

He shifted from her neck to take her breast into his mouth, and her eyes drifted closed as he suckled. Her body was all sensation, with a craving to reach the place she knew only he could take her.

She squeezed his member, eliciting a moan from his occupied mouth. "Does that hurt?"

"Nay, love," he said as he switched from one breast to the other. "Yer hand feels good, but if ye keep that up too long, 'twill all come to an end verra quickly."

A familiar need was building between her legs, and she thrashed, clutching his head to her breast, pressing her core hard against his hand. The sound of their breathing filled the room, the scent of her arousal mingling with Braeden's own unique one. Tightening all the muscles in her legs, she strained, trying desperately to feel once again the waves of pleasure he would bring to her.

"Dinna tense, lass. Relax."

"I can't help it, I'm so close." She tossed her head back and forth, reaching, stretching.

Braeden slid down her body and spread her legs apart. Before she even registered what he intended to do, he put his mouth *there* and licked her sensitive flesh. She sucked in a deep breath as everything in her body exploded. Throwing her head back, she dug her nails into his shoulders as he kept up his assault. Wave after wave of pleasure washed over her until she felt as though her heart would surely give out.

Before she recovered from his onslaught, he crawled up her body, and sliding his hands beneath her bottom to lift her, he thrust his hips forward into her moistness.

"Yes," she hissed, as she was pushed back against the headboard from the force of his entry.

He began the dance of lovers, sliding in and out, raising her response once again. "Braeden."

"Aye, lass." He nestled his head in her neck, biting and soothing the soft skin there. Once more he whispered words in Gaelic as he continued to stroke, flexing his hips as he moved within her.

His movements increased, bringing her once again to the place she longed to be. She licked the skin on his neck, loving the salty taste, inhaled the musky scent of his flesh.

Straining for a second time toward her release, she moved with him, both of their bodies frantic as they raced toward completion. Tilting her hips, she wrapped her legs around his waist, his pounding causing the headboard to bounce against the wall.

Sarah began to wail as her muscles clenched and her body was consumed with wave after wave of pleasure. Braeden covered her mouth and swallowed her cry as he stiffened and poured himself into her, gripping her shoulders tightly as he continued his ravishment. He threw his head back and groaned her name, then collapsed on top of her.

He immediately rolled to the side and pulled her to him,

their slick skin sliding against each other.

Sarah licked her dry lips and tried desperately to gain some air for her lungs. Her heart pounded wildly in rhythm with Braeden's. After several minutes their breathing slowed, and she turned her head. He stared at her, his piercing blue eyes telling her what she didn't want to know. Didn't want to consider. She closed her eyes and groaned.

She was in a great deal of trouble.

Chapter Eighteen

It was drawing near the end of their week in Inverness. Sarah had never been to the city at the mouth of the River Ness, and Braeden took a great deal of pleasure in showing her the area.

She'd purposely left her writing at the cottage. As lovely a setting as Inverness was for inspiration, she'd decided to give herself a true holiday. No disastrous road trip like before, no scrunching over paper and pen. Just the two of them enjoying what might very well be their last trip together.

She tried very hard to push that thought from her mind.

Soon she would have to tell him about her commitment in London. But for now, she wanted to pretend all was well. There was no expected letter for the expedition to Rome, no missive from her publisher on a book release demanding her attention in London.

They'd spent the week visiting shops and enjoying walks along the river. Sarah devoted the mornings to lying in bed, enjoying chocolate and oat cakes, and reading the morning newspaper. Braeden bought her several novels that she read while he met with a professor friend who also had an interest in early Roman civilization.

Then after a leisurely bath and dressing for the day, she was ready to meet her husband to see the sights. He was smart, attentive, humorous, and a wealth of information. The nights were even better. Braeden drew forth pleasure from her body she had never dreamed of. The pictures in Drake's book took on new meanings, and her blushes each morning as she greeted him in the light of day only brought deep chuckles from her husband.

Had she wished to be married, there could not have been a better man for her. Which, of course, was the problem.

Over a late dinner on the final night in Inverness, Braeden sipped brandy as he explained Scottish history. With one of his slim fingers running along the edge of the glass, he stared at the fireplace reflectively. "After the Battle of Culloden, the British reduced the power of the clan chiefs. That made it possible for outsiders to acquire a great deal of Scottish land."

She'd never known much about what her country had done to the Highlanders. It most likely had been covered by her governess, or perhaps in classes when she had attended Miss Baker's School for Young Ladies. But if it had, it would have been brief. The focus of the school had been on how to prepare oneself for life within the station into which the young ladies had been born.

Braeden continued. "These new owners evicted thousands of crofters, and that became known as the Clearances. Instead of small tenant subsidy farmers, they created large sheep-farming estates. That was when many left the Highlands for the Lowlands and America."

"Yet your family and the MacBrides seem to have survived."

His lips quirked in a slight smile. "Partially. We lost some land, but the area of the Highlands we occupy was not as appealing to the Sassenach."

Sarah nodded. "Ah. That was the name Liam called Sybil that started their disagreement. My sister broke their betrothal and left Bedlay to return home. The laird followed her."

"Aye. I've heard the story from Duncan. 'Tis quite a tale." He took a sip of his brandy and studied the glass. "But for the most part, my cousin kept his clan intact, and the crofters who Duncan couldn't find work for left for America. My brothers share their sheep farming, and my parents and sisters work at the castle."

"And you teach at university."

He regarded her cautiously. "And, hopefully, about to be part of a team on an expedition to Rome."

"Perhaps." Even though she had fought it, by the end of this trip she could no longer deny that she was deeply in love with her husband. If they continued to live together, especially with his wit, charm, and seductive ways, all that she had fought for would be lost.

No, as soon as his letter came she would be off to London, where Braeden could stop by to visit between excursions.

"What's the matter, love?" Braeden used his thumb to wipe a tear from the edge of Sarah's eye. Even though he'd thought they'd had a wonderful time on this trip, Sarah had seemed melancholy toward the end. Almost as if something were ending instead of them having the rest of their lives together. If anything had convinced him of the rightness of his marriage, it had been this time spent together. They suited. 'Twas as simple as that. The timing, and the way it had happened might not have been ideal, but there was no denying how well it had turned out.

The minor problem of dragging her around with him needed to be addressed, but he loved the lass, and although neither had spoken the words aloud, he kenned she loved him as well. It would be a good life.

"Are ye sad that our time here is over?"

She nodded, but looked away, avoiding his eyes which made him wonder if 'twere something else. They'd just finished another rousing session of lovemaking, and he was feeling quite drowsy. Despite his earlier reservations, he'd never acquired the French letters. Using something with his own wife that was generally reserved for mistresses seemed verra wrong. Hopefully, his seed didn't take, and they would not have the problem of raising a bairn in Rome.

He pulled Sarah's warm body against his and yawned. "We will need to be up early, lass, so I suggest we get some sleep."

"Yes. That's a good idea." She rolled over and turned her back to him, and he tugged her closer, the two of them tucked together like spoons in a drawer. Nuzzling the soft skin of her nape, he gave her a few soft kisses and then drifted off to sleep.

In the morning, Braeden felt the warmth from the sun bathing his face before he opened his eyes. Sunlight peeked over the edge of the windowsill, casting the room in an ethereal glow. Sarah had turned during the night and was now plastered over him, her bent leg bringing her knee very close to his morning erection. Her arm rested over his waist, and her bedtime braid had come loose, causing her silky locks to drape over his chest. He eased back and gazed down at her beloved face while he held her in his arms, and decided right then he would enjoy waking up, just this way, every morning for the rest of his life.

As much as he would enjoy staying like this for hours, they needed to get started on their journey home. Now that their time here had ended, he was anxious to know if the letter had finally arrived.

"Lass, 'tis time to get up." He kissed the soft hair on the crown of her head.

Sarah shifted and mumbled.

Unable to help himself, he slid his hand between them and caressed the warm breast crushed against his chest.

Sarah sighed and murmured his name.

Smiling, his hand moved farther down to tease the soft flesh between her legs.

Sarah pushed against his fingers and moaned.

"Darlin', if ye don't get your lovely arse out of this bed, we'll be here for another hour, and we need to get on the road."

Her eyes popped open and she laughed. "I wasn't asleep. I wanted to see how far you would go."

"Aye. I can tell ye how far I want to go, but we'll have to save that for another time." He patted her gently on her bottom. "Up with ye, now."

She rolled off him and stretched. "I shan't be long. Alice got everything ready last night. After a quick wash, I will have her help me dress, and we can have breakfast and go."

"*Ach*, no need to have Alice help ye. I can be yer lady's maid this morning."

She smirked. "Just keep in mind that you are helping me dress, not undress."

"I will try my best, lass." He winked at her and hopped from the bed.

After only a bit of touching and fondling while he helped Sarah dress, they made their way to the dining room for a light breakfast before leaving the inn. Alice supervised the loading of the trunks, and within an hour of rising they were saying good-bye to Inverness and headed home.

Home. Where he hoped at long last, good news awaited him.

He really should have a conversation with Sarah about what the expedition would mean for them, something he kept putting off. He had sensed her reluctance from the start, and rather than ruin the closeness they'd enjoyed on this trip, he would speak with her about it soon.

Verra soon.

She would have to make several decisions. Of course she would come with him, but would she insist on bringing her maid? And where would they live? The few expeditions he'd been on when he'd been a graduate student had been headed and staffed by single men, so there had been no women in the group.

It would probably be best to write to the committee when the information came through to see what provisions could be made for married persons. He remembered talking to an older professor at university who brought his wife and children on his expeditions. He had said whatever difficulties his wife had run into, she'd been able to straighten out.

He had confidence in Sarah. She had a good head on her shoulders and would handle whatever challenges they faced.

Sarah stared out the window as the carriage pulled up to the stone cottage on McKinnon land. She breathed a sigh of relief, more than happy to be free of the coach. With delays due to the weather, they'd spent several days on the journey home.

Braeden extended his hand to help her out, then wrapped his arm around her waist as her legs started to give out.

"'Twas a long journey."

"Yes. I'm afraid I feel as though I've been rocking back and forth for hours."

Feeling stronger, Sarah moved away from Braeden and started up the stairs toward the bedchamber. "Alice, please have a bath set up for me. I feel grimy from the road."

She'd barely closed the door when there was a whoop from Braeden and the sound of his footsteps pounding the stairs.

"Sarah! The letter arrived while we were gone." He burst into the room, waving a piece of foolscap, a wide grin on his face.

She sat on the edge of the bed, her mouth open. So the time had come. Relief mixed with an overwhelming sense of sadness gripped her. Their time together was almost over.

He would go on his expedition, and she would start her new life in London as an author. It was what she'd worked toward for years and was for the best.

She wanted to be her own person, not known only as Professor McKinnon's wife.

She worked up a slight smile. "It appears from your enthusiasm that you were granted a place on the expedition."

"Aye." He ran his fingers through his hair and looked as though he wanted to jump up and down like a child.

"Congratulations. I'm sure you will do a wonderful job."

His expression grew serious. "I know we just arrived, and ye are tired of being in the carriage, but I'm afraid we will have to leave within the next few days. I have a great deal of work to do before we go, so ye will have to prepare whatever it is ye think ye will need on yer own.

"I really dinna ken what type of clothing ye need, but I'm sure there are shops in the village not too far from where we will be outside of Rome." He glanced down at the paper, smiling again. "'Tis times like this that I wished I had a valet to prepare that part of it for me."

"I'm not going." Her voice barely rose above a whisper.

"The professor I met with in Inverness had been on an expedition with a man who had his wife with him. He gave me some ideas of how this will all work—"

Sarah cleared her throat. "I'm not going, Braeden."

He stopped and stared. "What do ye mean?"

She took a deep breath, determined to get this over with as quickly as possible. Then she could retire to her sister's house and cry her eyes out. "I have my own commitments. In London."

His eyes narrowed. "What are ye talking about?"

She stood and paced, wringing her hands. "I'm sorry. I should have told you long before now, but the time never seemed right." She stopped and drew in a deep breath. "I am about to have a book published, and my publisher insists on me being there."

The paper in his hand drifted to the floor as he stared at her, his mouth open, his eyebrows drawn together. "What?"

"It's simple, really." Unable to stand still, she resumed her pacing. "All that writing that I do. I'm sorry, but I lied to you. That writing wasn't in a journal, it is another book that my publisher is waiting for."

Braeden shook his head in disbelief. "You wrote a book?"

"Yes."

"What type of book?"

She raised her chin, her eyes narrowing. "Why?" This was the point in their conversation she had always dreaded. Her heart pounded and she hugged her middle. Here was where he would laugh and dismiss her work.

"Because I…I want to know."

She closed her eyes briefly. "Romance."

Braeden opened and closed his mouth several times. She held her breath, waiting for laughter. Finally, he grinned. "That's wonderful."

She blew out the breath she held. "You think so?"

"Of course I think so. 'Tis verra hard to write a book. To make up a story from beginning to end and write it all down. 'Tis a great accomplishment, and I'm verra proud of ye."

Sarah burst into tears.

"What's the matter, lass?" He pulled her into his arms and held her close as tears of relief fell.

"I thought you would laugh at me."

He drew back and regarded her. "I thought ye kenned me better than that. I have a great deal of respect for books and the authors who write them."

"Even romance?" She giggled.

"Even romance, love." He patted her on her backside. "Now hurry yerself upstairs and get yer packing done. We don't have much time to prepare for Rome."

"What?"

"We have a lot to do before we leave. I won't have time to learn what accommodations will be made for ye before we leave, so we best be prepared for anything."

"Wait a minute." Sarah waved her hand in front of his face to get his attention. "I just told you, I'm not going with you to Rome."

"Why not?"

"Braeden, I know you have a lot on your mind, but you can't tell me you forgot the conversation we just had about my book."

"Nay. I remember it well. 'Tis proud I am of ye."

She took him by the hand and led him to the bed where they both sat. "I have to be in London when my book releases. It is in the contract I signed with my publisher. My book will release very soon. Therefore, I cannot go to Rome because I must be in London."

He stared at her as if she had just announced plans to join the circus. "Yer my wife. Ye go where yer husband goes. I'm going to Rome."

She drew herself up. "And I'm going to London."

He smacked his fist into his open palm. "This is my work."

"And this is my work." She leaned in until they were nose to nose.

Braeden threw his hands into the air and rose. "I'm verra happy for ye to have finished a book, and managed to find someone to publish it for ye. But now yer a wife, and you need to put aside your hobby and go with me on my expedition."

She reared back as if he had slapped her. "My hobby!" No doubt the people at Dundas Castle stopped their work at the screech that came from her mouth.

"Aye. A hobby that ye can put aside now that yer married."

"That is precisely why I didn't want a husband."

"Well, 'tis too late now, lass, cause ye do have one."

Her not-quite-recovered head would probably explode from the anger that surged through her. A hobby! He might as well have laughed at her. But instead of feeling the hurt she thought that attitude would elicit, she was so blasted mad, she could pommel his face.

"I refuse to argue with you, Professor McKinnon. Alice will pack my belongings, but I can assure you it will be to return to my sister's home to await word from my publisher on when he requires my presence in London." She swept past him, reaching the door before she realized this was their bedroom.

She turned back. "Please leave me so I may tend to my duties."

"Yer duty is with yer husband."

A knock at the door startled them both. "Yes," Sarah said.

Alice opened the door. "A message just came from Bedlay Castle that your mother has arrived and is requesting you visit." The maid's eyes darted between the two of them and quickly hurried away.

Sarah raised her chin. "If you will excuse me, Professor,

I will have Alice finish packing my belongings. If I may use the carriage to return to Bedlay, I would greatly appreciate it."

He gave her a slight bow, his features tightened into a mask. "As you wish." He turned on his heel and left the room, not even bothering to close the door behind him. His footsteps as they padded away beat in rhythm with her pounding heart.

"Alice!" She shouted from the doorway. She swiped at the liquid on her cheeks. She must be overwarm, and that was perspiration dripping from her chin. Smiling brightly, she looked around, making note of her things mingled with Braeden's.

Don't think about that.

Damn that blasted heat, her face was wet again, and shaky hands wiped her cheeks once more. And where in heaven's name was Alice? She needed to hurry. Not sure why, but nevertheless, there it was. "Alice!"

The woman entered the room. "Is everything all right, my lady?"

"Perfect!" Her smile could light up the entire downstairs portion of Bedlay castle.

"Are you feeling well, my lady?"

"I feel wonderful, absolutely marvelous. Now we must pack."

"Pack? We just arrived."

"We must hurry and pack so we can return to Bedlay Castle."

"Return to Bedlay Castle?"

"Really, Alice, has your hearing begun to deteriorate? You seem to be repeating everything I say."

"If I may be so bold, my lady, your mother merely

requested that you come for a visit. I believe she had tea in mind." The maid looked at her, but when she opened her mouth to speak, she quickly closed it. Then she gave a slight curtsy. "Certainly, my lady. If that is what you wish."

"I do."

Damnation, why did she use those two words? And why was it so blasted hot in here that the perspiration kept dripping down her cheeks?

Chapter Nineteen

August 11, 1817
Dear Sarah,

This note is to inform you that we have arrived at our destination and have set up our camp. My direction is below in the event you need to contact me. This is where all of our mail goes to be collected once a week and delivered to the site.

Professor Braeden McKinnon
Piazza Venezia
Genzano Nuova, Italy
Braeden

Braeden stared at the words. There was so much more in his heart. His heavy heart. He'd hated the way they'd parted. Anger on both sides. Of course he understood her pride in her accomplishment. Hadn't he told her he was proud of her, too? But he was the man in this marriage, and a wife went with her husband. Even the Bible dictated that.

The morning she'd left the stone cottage she had appeared ready to shatter into a million pieces. Had he reached out and touched her, he was sure she would have crumbled. Yet, with her head held high, she had sailed out the door, determination in her every step. He had followed her to the carriage, but stopped when she never turned around, realizing she was not going to change her mind. With his duties awaiting him on the dig, he had no choice but to let her go.

He folded the missive and added it to the stack of letters leaving today to be carried to town for mailing. The responsibility for his part of the expedition was on his shoulders. He'd fought for this, and now he had a job to do. The distraction of his wife needed to be put aside.

If there were to be any changing of one's mind it must come from her. Shaking himself from his malaise, he grabbed his notes and a pencil and headed to the excavation site.

When Sarah had arrived at the castle it was to Sybil's surprise. The only thing she'd shared with her twin and mother was that Braeden had accepted the expedition to Rome, and she was staying behind to await her publisher's summons.

There had been a moment of absolute joy when she told her mother about her book. Dabbing at her eyes, she had hugged Sarah and told her over and over again how proud she was of her. Then she had immediately chastised her for not going with Braeden.

Did no one understand how important this was to her?

As was her mother's way, after her initial outburst, she hadn't pried, but watched her carefully for days. Sybil, on the other hand, had asked flat out what the devil she thought she was doing. It had caused the first serious rift between the twins. But Sarah had refused to be drawn into the argument. It was her decision, after all, and she'd made it.

> *August 27, 1817*
> *Dear Braeden,*
>
> *Thank you for the information. I have put your letter in safekeeping in the event it becomes necessary to send word to you.*
>
> *No letter from my publisher as yet, but I am enjoying time with my mother. She is sorry she did not get to meet you. Perhaps another time. Mother is already madly in love with Sybil's babes.*
>
> *Sarah*

Sarah stared glumly out the window at the darkening sky. She clamped her arms around her waist and rubbed her stomach to ward off the pain of her courses. Despite being late this month, their last week together had not produced a babe. She'd tried to convince herself she had been relieved when she'd spotted the specks of blood on her sheet that morning.

It had almost worked.

"Sarah, Alice said you were under the weather. Is everything all right?" Her mother stuck her head in the room after tapping lightly on the bedroom door.

"Yes. It is just my monthlies. You know how painful they sometimes are."

"Ah, yes. Indeed I do. I always found it necessary to spend a day or two in bed. I must admit I am more than pleased to be done with it all." She smiled at her daughter as she continued farther into the room and perched on the edge of the mattress.

"Of course, having six children did allow me to escape the trouble each month during the times I carried my babes."

September 16, 1817
Dear Sarah,
   The days are hot and the nights are long.
   Braeden

When he couldn't think of anything else to say, he folded the letter and put it onto the stack to be driven into the village and sent on its way. Sadly, there was quite a bit more to add, but some things were better left unspoken. He was still hurt and confused by Sarah's refusal to come with him.

Perhaps he shouldn't have referred to her book as a hobby, but his work was important. He had spent years of his life being educated and preparing for this expedition. How important was a romance novel? It was wonderful that she wrote one, and he was truly happy for her, but to compare the two was ludicrous.

However, his work was exciting—by his standard, anyway. He imagined most people would find it tedious and boring, examining bits and pieces of life and recording them. But discovering unknown facts about societies from many years ago was what kept him pushing himself day after day.

Truth be known, he also pushed himself in hopes that he would be able to sleep, and not spend his time staring at the tiny tear in the ceiling of his canvas tent and wondering where it had all gone wrong. They had the start of a good life together. Passion, common interests, and love. He loved her. It was that simple. And despite Sarah never saying the words, he kenned that she loved him, too.

However, the fact remained she had rejected him and their marriage, so he would just have to put it all behind him and allow his work to consume him as it had done for years. 'Twas past time for him to stop brooding like a love-sick lad and accept things as they were.

October 3, 1817
Dear Braeden,

I took the twins on a stroll today in their pram. It amazed me how heavy two little babes are when one is pushing them uphill.

Duncan and Margaret came for dinner last evening. I enjoyed seeing my friend once again, but I found it necessary to retire early when my head began to ache.

Still no word from my publisher.
Sarah

She chewed on the end of her pencil. If she continued to write to Braeden, she would never accept her new life. She refused to abandon what she had worked so hard for, and received so much satisfaction from. Her second book was finished to her liking, and she would be proud to personally hand it to her publisher when she returned to London.

Her mother was very understanding of her need to express herself by writing, but made it quite clear she disapproved of Sarah putting her books before her husband. Everywhere she turned, it seemed she found acceptance mixed with censure.

October 21, 1817
Dear Sarah,
 All those days conjugating Latin verbs and keeping imperfect and pluperfect tenses straight has made this assignment so much more enjoyable.
 Braeden

"Ye writing a letter again, lad?" Kevin MacGregor, a large Scot who was part of the expedition, stood a few feet from him, hands on his hips, his body blocking the sun. Although Braeden was an integral part of the team, he'd yet to get some of the older members to address him as anything other than "lad." "Have ye a lass at home?"

"Aye. My wife."

"Ah. 'Tis a hard thing to leave yer woman behind." Without invitation, the man sat on the rock next to him and raised a flint to his pipe, inhaling deeply. "My wife always traveled with me. 'Twas hard when the bairns were little."

Braeden snorted. MacGregor's wife had traveled with the man even when they had bairns. With Sarah so concerned about her book and her publisher, there would likely never be bairns for them. A husband and wife needed to be in the same place in order to do what it was that married people did to bring bairns into the world.

His time with Sarah and their lovemaking had been vastly different from his prior encounters. They'd assuaged his lust, but at the same time had left him with a sense of something missing. Now he kenned his love for his wife had made their time together powerful and satisfying. He'd not been left with the emptiness that had marked his prior beddings. He wanted that fulfillment again. Over and over.

There was only one woman who could do that.

He came back to himself when he realized MacGregor was still talking.

"Even though my Bessie trailed along with me, I came to believe 'twas not the best life for a family." He shook his head. "'Twas hard on her."

As he nodded at the man, not really listening to his words, Braeden continued to ruminate. 'Twas best to push thoughts of Sarah from his mind. He'd wanted this spot on the expedition and had worked hard to get it. His focus was best placed in his work. Where he had always felt secure and confident, and dinna second guess his every move.

November 1, 1817
Dear Braeden,
I was unsuccessful with Latin. English, Italian,

and French were enough of a challenge for me.
  Sarah

Sarah tossed the pen down. This was utterly ridiculous. There was absolutely no reason for them to be writing back and forth and saying nothing. Everything she wanted to say was locked inside her, where she hoped it would die a slow death and not trouble her anymore. So far she'd received two notes from her publisher about delays in the printing. The longer it took for her book to be published, the more she missed Braeden.

There, perhaps she hadn't said it out loud, but she'd thought it out loud. She missed him. Missed the facts he spewed at her from nowhere. Missed his smile, his silly jokes, his kisses. She missed his lovemaking most of all.

She set the letter aside and walked to the window. The Highlands was such a beautiful place. Mysterious, and in some ways frightening, at the same time. It was no wonder there were so many tales of ghostly happenings. Yet with her emotions being mysterious and frightening, it seemed this was where she belonged.

Sybil seemed happy in her marriage and had settled in quite nicely to the Scottish way of life. Whatever issues she and Liam had at the beginning had been resolved. As time went on, Sarah grew more uncomfortable in their presence. The love they shared was so strong and beautiful it made her ache.

I could have that.

It had been there for the taking, but she'd refused it, and had sent her husband away with the notion that her book was more important than him. She had told him that. The pride of seeing her name in print on the cover of a book in London bookstores, and the nonsense about being an independent person, along with the reception her publisher planned, had all meant more to her than the man she loved.

She missed him so much. Despite her mental machinations, it came down to the simple fact that she loved Braeden. The uncomfortable idea that she'd made a mistake had begun to take root.

As the tears slid down her cheeks, she could not convince herself that the room was merely too hot and this was perspiration.

"Sarah, join us for tea?" The sound of Sybil's voice jerked her from her self-pity. Wiping her cheeks quickly before she turned, she said, "Yes, of course."

They joined their mother in Sybil's sitting room where a tray of cups and saucers, along with small cakes and tiny sandwiches, sat on a low table in front of a settee and two chairs. This was the babes' nap time, so the women generally gathered for conversation over tea.

"Are Lady MacBride and the girls not joining us?" Sarah took the cup of steaming liquid from Sybil's hand.

"No. They have gone into town."

The Dowager Duchess of Manchester eyed her daughter over her teacup with a steely look that Sarah had only seen a few times in her life. "My dear, when are you going to stop this foolishness and join your husband?"

That look still had the power to cause her stomach to flutter. Not in the way Braeden's lazy smile could, but as if she were a child caught with one of Cook's tarts clutched in her hand before dinner.

"What do you mean?" She opted for ignorance, knowing

full well that would not work with her mother.

"Your place is with Braeden, and you know that. I had hoped I raised you girls better than to put anything before your marriage. I am quite sure that was not the example your father and I provided for you."

Sybil stood and shook out her skirts. "I think I will check on the babes." She squeezed Sarah's shoulder in support before she left the room.

Her mother reached her hand out and pulled Sarah down alongside her on the settee. "It is very obvious to this mother's eye that you are miserable, Sarah. I know your marriage came about in an unusual way, but Sybil and Liam both assure me you and Braeden care very deeply for each other. Is this book of yours—of which I am extremely proud—more important than your husband?"

"Yes. Well, no." She jumped up from the settee. "I honestly do not know anymore."

"What I do not understand is what is keeping you away from Braeden. Unless I've been grossly misled, Rome is not exactly the ends of the earth, and I'm sure somewhere in that city you can find pen and paper to continue your writing."

"It's not just the writing, Mother. My publisher is holding a reception for me. He has set up newspaper interviews to make my book known. He would like me to visit bookstores and autograph my books for readers."

"I see. So your pride is involved."

Sarah gaped at her mother. "It is not that at all!"

She raised her brows. "No?"

"No. Well not really. At least I don't think so."

"Then when Miss Austen's books went into print, she also had a reception and waltzed around London, visiting bookstores so everyone could admire her work?"

Sarah raised her chin. "I have no idea."

"I do. She did not. Miss Austen leads a very quiet life in the country." She reached for her cup and took a sip of tea.

"Would it truly be so difficult for you to forego the reception and travel to Rome and possibly have to live in a tent? Where is the adventurer I raised who was always looking for the next escapade?" Her mother's warm smile eased the pain in her heart. "Just think of how inspiring Rome might be."

"It's not only the reception and all the rest of it. Braeden referred to my writing as a 'hobby.' He thinks his work is more important than mine."

"He is a man, my dear." Her mother smiled. "Everything they do is more important than anything us women can do. Like it or not, that is the way of the world. Although I have yet to meet this son-in-law, I somehow do not think a man you love would dismiss your work so easily. I have a feeling he was angry and hurt when those words left his mouth."

Sarah sat with her hands in her lap, musing over her mother's words. Truth be known, she was not happy, and indeed, the idea of being an independent woman with the status of author didn't appeal to her as much as it once had.

Not that she had any intention of not writing. Writing was not something she liked to do, it was something she *had* to do. It was as much a part of her life as breathing and eating. Mother was right. No doubt she could find paper and pens in Rome.

Was she truly thinking of joining Braeden? As the idea grew, the excitement began to build. How she longed to feel his arms around her. To inhale his scent of leather, horses, and Braeden. To once again have the pleasure of their lovemaking.

As if a great weight was lifted from her shoulders, she smiled her first true smile since Braeden had left. She would see her husband again! They would make love, talk, go for lazy walks, hold each other during the long nights, and make plans for their future.

This very day she would dash off a note to her publisher, along with her completed manuscript. She would advise him of her new status as a married lady, and as such, any decisions had to be made with that in mind. Right now the decision about her returning to London any time soon had been made. He would have to carry on without her.

"Mother, I will do it."

Her mother cupped her cheeks. "You are making the right decision." She kissed her on the top of her head. "Be happy, my daughter."

All right, Braeden. I'm on my way.

Chapter Twenty

Once Sarah had made up her mind, she found any little impediment to her departure impossible to deal with. And there were many. The first arrived the next morning when Alice claimed she could not have her wardrobe ready for travel for at least three days.

"What takes so long? All we have to do is put everything into the trunk and have someone lug it to the carriage."

Alice was horrified. "No, my lady. Many of your gowns have to be cleaned before they can be packed. And I have items I've been holding to launder. It will take at least three days to set it all to rights and then pack."

Frustrated at the delay, Sarah pulled on her breeches, shirt, and a jacket, then headed to the stables. The day was cool and damp, but she needed the exercise. She would be ready for a visit to Bedlam if she didn't clear her mind.

What had she been thinking? Years of rejecting overtures from men was nothing compared to sending her husband away thinking she had no use for him. As if her books meant more to her than he did. She cringed, remembering his face when they'd parted ways.

She loved the man, plain and simple. She loved his laugh, his wit, his caring, his lazy smile. There were so many things about Braeden that she loved, it would take a full day to list them all. But if she couldn't spur Alice along, she would have three days to catalog his attributes while bemoaning her folly in sending him off.

"Good morning, my lady. Are ye off for a ride?" The stableboy set the strap he was working on aside and rubbed his palms on his breeches.

"Yes. Might you please tack Ambrose for me?"

The boy pushed back the brim of his cap and scratched his hairline. "Are ye sure, my lady? I can find a nice, calm mare for ye to ride."

She grinned at the boy's reluctance to let her ride a horse he deemed unsuitable for a lady. "I am not in the mood for a nice, calm ride. I've ridden her a few times and I find her very spirited." She raised her hand as he began to protest. "I want a spirited animal. I can assure you, I am quite capable of handling her."

He shook his head, most likely remembering when Liam had brought her back to the castle, unconscious from being thrown. Of course, that wasn't the only time in her life she'd been abruptly separated from her horse's back, but the last thing she wanted today was a meek animal plodding along. She needed speed to ease her restless anxiety.

The wind whipped through her hair, making quick work of the heavy braid resting on her back. With her locks streaming behind her, she flew over the land surrounding

Bedlay and headed to Dundas. Perhaps if she looked at the stone cottage once again she would feel closer to Braeden.

How she must have hurt him. From the beginning he'd been nothing but kind and thoughtful. He'd even held back from disclosing that she'd accidentally married them until she was with her sister to help soften the blow. Everything the man had done since she'd met him had been considerate. Who else would accompany her, a complete stranger, on a journey that had caused him a weeks-long delay?

The outside of the cottage looked sad and forlorn, as if mourning its master and mistress, holding its breath as it awaited their return. Sitting on the horse's back staring at the place she and Braeden had lived for such a short time didn't bring her closer to him. It only reinforced the anxiety to be on her way, to feel his arms around her, making her feel loved and protected.

Did Braeden love her? A kernel of fear nudged at her that he would not have left if he had. Then she pushed that notion away. He was a man committed to his work. Once she'd told him where her priorities lay, she'd left him no choice. She would have to reconcile herself to the fact that his work would always come first.

Nudging the horse lightly, she turned in the direction of Dundas. A visit with Margaret might improve her mood.

Heavy mist shrouded the castle as she approached at a full gallop. The structure seemed to rise from the ground in front of her, bathed in mystery and lore like a pirate's ship emerging from a fog.

"Good morning, my lady." The older man who oversaw the stables at Dundas greeted her, unmoved by her appearance in breeches and skidding into the stable as if her hair were on fire.

"Good morning," she returned. By the time she slid from the horse's back, both she and Ambrose were panting and covered with a fine sheen of perspiration.

"I'm afraid I gave her a good run. I think that made her happy, but she needs a hard rubdown."

He tugged at the brim of his cap and gave her a gap-tooth grin. "'Tis happy I am to take care of 'er for ye."

Knowing the animal was in good hands, she strode to the front door. It amazed her how freeing breeches were. She was able to ride better and walk faster. Perhaps she could get away with wearing them when she went to Rome.

Rome. Where Braeden worked, thinking his wife placed him second behind her books. Once again she wished to be on her way—immediately. Shaking off the gloomy thoughts, she opened the massive door to the great hall and entered.

"**N**o! I refuse to accept that." Sarah glared at Liam, her tiny body all anger and tension pitted against the massive size of the laird.

He drew his brows together. "The roads are still too dangerous for ye to travel today. The constant rain has turned everything into a muddle. I cannae allow ye to journey now, 'tis not safe, lass."

"I don't believe this!" She paced back and forth, waving her hands in the air. "It has been more than a week since I decided to go to Rome, and here I am, trunks packed, ready to leave, and now the weather is uncooperative."

"Dear, you must settle down. Nothing can be done about

the weather. Come have a cup of tea." Mother poured the steaming liquid into a cup and held it out to her.

"You always think tea will solve everything, Mother. Well, it won't solve this." She stamped her foot and scowled.

The dowager duchess raised her chin. "If you were a few years younger, my girl, I would send you to your room until you located your good manners."

Knowing she was behaving like a recalcitrant child, Sarah fled the room, swiping at the tears rolling down her cheeks. No one understood. She had to get to Rome. To Braeden. All the pent-up love and desire she'd been tamping down for months had to be let out before she exploded. Heading to the front door, she grabbed her cape from the hook and left the castle.

The blasted rain continued to pour down. The long-abandoned moat surrounding the castle would soon be filled and able to be put to good use if the torrential downpours didn't stop. Soaked through her cape to her gown and even her skin, she picked her way through the puddles and walked to the stables.

The familiar smells of animals and hay calmed her nerves somewhat. She retrieved a soggy handkerchief from her cape pocket and wiped her face—partially rain water and partially salted tears. She leaned her forehead against Ambrose, the tears continuing to drop.

"I want to leave. I want to go to Rome. Please, God, make it stop raining."

The sound of a horse's hooves pounding on the path to the stable, splashing water, plodding through mud and puddles, had her once more quickly wiping the tears from her face. She took a deep breath and turned with a bright smile to greet the person who wasn't afraid of a little rain.

The man's head was lowered, his hat pulled down over his forehead. He ducked as he rode into the stable then looked up, his eyes searching the space. Sarah's breath hitched and she took two steps forward, not believing her eyes.

Braeden sat staring at her for a minute, then, his eyes never leaving hers, threw his leg over the horse and hit the floor. He strode up to her as if he'd expected her to be standing there in this very spot. Her mouth dropped open, and she shook her head, quite sure she'd managed to conjure up an illusion.

"Braeden?"

"Aye, lass."

With a cry, she threw herself into his arms, sobbing and trying to speak all at once. He rubbed her back and held her, murmuring to her in Gaelic. His warmth and scent surrounded her, making her dizzy with relief and joy. He was here! All this time she was anxious to leave, and he had been on his way to her.

Before she could ask even one question, he gripped her face and covered her mouth with his warm one, nibbling, tasting, soothing. Once more dizziness threatened to hold her captive. She held firmly to his muscled arms as he shifted her head, taking the kiss so deep she felt it to her toes.

When he finally pulled them apart, he held her shoulders and smiled that lazy smile she loved so much.

"What are you doing here?"

"I'm home, lass. As much as I wanted the Rome expedition, it dinna matter with you here."

"You gave it up?" She was stunned.

"Aye. I turned my position over to another team member

who'd been itching to take my place."

"But…"

"I dinna want to stand out here wet and cold, but what I have to say needs to be said privately and quickly." He held her hands to his lips and kissed each knuckle. "Ye are my wife. I love ye, lass, and although I ken yer books are important to ye, I'm thinking we can work on a compromise. Being apart we have no chance of having a happy marriage.

"And 'tis what I want above all else. My work is verra important to me, but I'm just as happy in the classroom as I am digging in the dirt. I'm sure I can secure a position in one of yer London universities. Kenning ye are at home waiting for me each night makes the classroom the better choice."

"You will be surprised to learn my bags have been packed for days."

"Aye. Returning to London?"

"No. I was about to embark on a trip to Rome. I was made to understand a very handsome, intelligent, and lovable man, who just happened to be my husband, was residing in a tent there."

His eyes widened. "You were coming to me?"

She nodded, then burst into laughter, soon joined by Braeden.

"*Ach*, lass. We are a pair." He tucked a curl behind her ear. "Nay. Expedition sites are no place for a wife, or the bairn I hope to add to our family soon." He cupped her cheeks. "I love you, Sarah."

She nodded. "I know. And I love you."

"Now we need to get out of these wet clothes before we both end up with an ague."

She accepted his arm and hung on tightly as they made

their way out of the stable, back into the pouring rain. Holding hands, they raced to the castle.

Once they reached the entrance she looked at him under lowered eyelashes. "I have a bedroom."

He grinned. "Aye, lass. I like the sound of that." He pushed open the heavy door and waved her in. "Lead the way, wife."

B raeden rolled off Sarah and tugged her close to his side. They both lay sprawled on top of the counterpane, trying to catch their breath. After a brief introduction to the lass's mother, and a quick hello to a stunned Liam and Sybil, Sarah had dragged him upstairs to her bedchamber.

He'd no sooner removed his wet clothes and dropped them into a pile on the floor than he stripped Sarah of her clothing, then tumbled them both onto the bed. They spent the next hour refreshing their memories of each other's bodies and what they could do to bring and receive pleasure.

"*Ach*, lass. I missed ye in so many ways, but surely this way the most." He played with a lock of her hair, raising it to his nose to sniff at the familiar scent of her soap.

Sarah shifted and rested her head on her hand. "Are you sure you've done the right thing in giving up the expedition? You worked so hard for it, and waited so long to have the opportunity."

He moved so he faced her. "'Tis not a life for a married man. Other men have done it, but I'd always kenned when I married that I would not want to drag my wife and bairns from place to place. Although I never expected to marry this soon, 'tis what I want. Ye are more important to me than any expedition."

One lone tear tracked from her eyes. "Despite being reluctant to live in a tent, I was prepared to join you in Rome."

"And for that I am grateful. But 'tis for the best. When the next semester begins, I'll seek a teaching post in Oxford or Cambridge. I have a few contacts."

"No, Braeden. I want you to return to Edinburgh. You were happy there."

"What about your book?"

"I've already written to my publisher. There is no need for me to be in London. I can write in Edinburgh and mail my manuscripts off."

"I love ye, lass." He gave her a teasing glance. "Until I can return to teaching, I have a great deal of research to do for my book."

"Book? You're writing a book?"

"Aye. I plan to use it for my students."

She sat up, her eyes eager. "I can help you with that."

"Aye. Ye can. We can work on it together."

She grew serious. "I never want you to regret your decision."

"Nay. When I make up my mind to something, 'tis done. I love teaching, so 'tis no hardship to return to university."

"Where will we live?"

"If yer sure about living in Edinburgh, I'll send a letter to my department head to expect us soon. I have a house near the university. 'Tis a small place, but 'twill suffice until we can find something more suitable. He kissed her gently on her pert nose.

When they finally left the bedroom the next morning, they met with the rest of the family for breakfast. No doubt understanding their need for time alone together, Sybil had arranged to have their dinner the previous evening delivered to their door.

They'd eaten the roasted chicken, bread, cheese, and bottle of wine naked, sitting cross-legged on the bed. Sarah had never enjoyed a meal more.

"How nice to finally get to speak with my son-in-law," her mother said as she extended her hand to Braeden.

"Aye, Yer Grace, 'tis a pleasure to speak with ye as well. I see now from where Sarah and Sybil get their beauty."

Mother's eyes flashed with humor as she regarded him. "And I see why another of my daughters fell in love with a Scottish man. You spew forth blarney much like the Irish do."

Braeden laughed. "Nay. I am telling the truth."

He pulled out a chair for Sarah, and they joined the rest at the table.

Liam scooped eggs onto his plate. "Now that yer here, and we can stop listening to yer wife complain about the delays to reach you..." He winked in Sarah's direction. "What are the two of ye planning on doing?"

Braeden took Sarah's hand. "We will be off to Edinburgh. I will resume my teaching post, and Sarah will help me with the book I'm writing on Ancient Rome."

"That is an excellent compromise, children," her mother said. "And I would love to visit the wonderful city of

Edinburgh." She added, "Sometime in the future, of course."

Braeden leaned over and kissed Sarah briefly on the lips. Softly, so no one heard him except her, he said, "Thank God yer mum is as smart as she is pretty."

Discover more from Callie Hutton...

THE ELUSIVE WIFE
THE DUKE'S QUANDARY
THE LADY'S DISGRACE
THE BARON'S BETRAYAL
THE HIGHLANDER'S CHOICE

Acknowledgments

As always, many thanks to my fabulous and hard-working editor, Erin Molta, who knows how I love to switch tenses in the middle of a paragraph.

Thank you to The Beau Monde, a group of wonderfully talented authors who share their expertise on everything Regency.

Thank you to my brainstorming partner and beta reader, Doug—who only reads romance because I write it.

About the Author

USA Today bestselling author of *The Elusive Wife*, Callie Hutton writes both Western Historical and Regency romance, with "historic elements and sensory details" (*The Romance Reviews*). She also pens an occasional contemporary or two. Callie lives in Oklahoma with several rescue dogs, two adult children, and daughter-in-law (thankfully all not in the same house), and her top cheerleader husband of thirty-eight years. She also recently welcomed twin grandsons to her ever expanding family. Callie loves to hear from readers, and would welcome you as a "friend" on Facebook. You can contact her through her website: www.calliehutton.com, or write her directly at calliehutton11@gmail.com